A Completely Different Place

Also by Perry Nodelman:

The Same Place but Different

By Perry Nodelman and Carol Matas:

Of Two Minds

More Minds

A Completely Different Place

Perry Nodelman

SIMON & SCHUSTER BOOKS FOR YOUNG READERS

SIMON & SCHUSTER BOOKS FOR YOUNG READERS
An imprint of Simon & Schuster Children's Publishing Division
1230 Avenue of the Americas, New York, New York 10020
Copyright © 1997 by Perry Nodelman
All rights reserved including the right of reproduction
in whole or in part in any form.
SIMON & SCHUSTER BOOKS FOR YOUNG READERS
is a trademark of Simon & Schuster.
Book design by Paul Zakris
The text of this book is set in 12-point Janson Text.
Printed and bound in the United States of America
First Edition
10 9 8 7 6 5 4 3 2 1

Library of Congress Cataloging-in-Publication Data

Nodelman, Perry.
    A completely different place / by Perry Nodelman.
    p.   cm.
    Sequel to: The same place but different.
    Summary: Johnny Nesbit returns to Stranger country with his former
classmate Cheryl to try to save a group of kidnapped children from the nasty
fairies.
    [1. Fairies—Fiction. 2. Fantasy.] I. Title.
    PZ7.N67175Co 1997 [Fic]—dc20 96-34183 CIP AC
    ISBN 0-689-80836-4

For Dorothy and Lonny Nodelman,
whose children never had to depend
on the kindness of strangers

Last winter, things were different. Last winter, things got weird around here. I don't mean your normal everyday weird. It wasn't just UFO sightings or sheep with two heads or potatoes that looked like Elvis. It was big-time weird.

It started when my baby sister, Andrea, stopped smiling and didn't do anything but sit in her infant seat and stare into space and poop in her diapers. My parents felt so bad about it that they turned into these zombies who never talked to each other and did nothing but yell at me. And as if that wasn't bad enough, it was hockey season, and my so-called friends had no time for anything but body-checking.

I hate body-checking. I hate hockey.

And then a window suddenly appeared in a hill down by the Monkey Paths in Churchill Drive Park, and inside the hill was a woman I used to know who was supposed to be dead. For a dead person she sure could talk a lot. She told me that the sick baby in my house wasn't really Andrea. It was a beer-guzzling creature just pretending to be Andrea. A Stranger. These Strangers were invading our world, and if I wanted to get Andrea back, I had to go to their country to get her. Oh, and by the way, I also had to save the entire known world from total disaster and annihilation. Me, little old John Nelson Nesbit.

Well, I did it. It was really no big deal. I did it, and things went back to normal.

Just normal, not perfect. There were still politicians. There were still Language Arts teachers. And there seemed to be lots of kids disappearing from the neighborhood—little kids and big kids, just somehow wandering off and never being heard of again.

But this is the nineties, right? Civilization is in decline. Nobody helps old ladies across the street anymore. Language Arts teachers are allowed to torture their prisoners with grammar and poetry on a daily basis. Kids disappear without a trace and are never seen again. You've got to expect stuff like that. It's just normal.

And my life was normal again, too. Blissfully, boringly normal. And then, one night . . .

One

"JOHNNY! JOHNNEEE NESSSSBITTTT! COME TO ME! COME TO ME, ME, MEEEEEE!"

The voice was above me, below me, behind me. It filled the world. It *was* the world. I couldn't escape it.

It was somebody I knew, but who? I was just about to figure out who the voice belonged to when the face suddenly appeared.

To begin with, it was just a pinpoint of light off in the distance—so small I wasn't even sure it *was* a face. Then it grew. It went from nothing to gigantic in about two seconds—and when I say gigantic, I mean gigantic. That was one big face. By the time it got close to me, my whole body was about the same size as its nose. If it got any closer, I'd be wearing that nose like an umbrella.

The gigantic brown eyes that hung there over that gigantic nose stared at me for a moment or two. Then the gigantic nose took a breath and nearly sucked me into its cavernous darkness. Then the gigantic lips opened, and I could see the gigantic teeth glistening right in front of my own puny little face. And I could hear the voice booming out of that gigantic mouth like thunder.

"JOHNNY!" it said again. "COME TO ME, PLEASE COME TO MEEEEE!"

At which point, I'm glad to say, I woke up.

I lay there in the dark, shivering and sweating like crazy. Talk about your crazy nightmares.

After a while, my heart stopped pounding quite so fast, and I started to think a little more clearly. That voice, and that face. They were familiar, all right.

It was the eyes, those big brown eyes. As I lay there remembering the imploring way they had stared at me, it suddenly came to me. I knew who it was. The eyes belonged to Cheryl Zennor, a girl who used to be in my class. A girl I hardly knew.

That confused me. Why would I have a dream about Cheryl Zennor? I'd talked to her twice, maybe, and that was just because she happened to be the one standing there in the hall when I needed to ask someone about what particular dumb homework assignment I'd managed to forget to do for that particular day.

As for being scared by her, well, that was like being scared by the Cookie Monster. By a cookie. By a cookie crumb. Cheryl was this really quiet person who hardly ever said anything to anybody. She wouldn't hurt a fly. In a one-on-one fight, the fly would probably win.

It was those sad cow eyes of hers. They made her look like the perfect victim, and bullies couldn't resist. Jason Garrett was at her all the time. Sitting in the desk behind her so he could stick his pencil in her back during class. Coming up to her in the hall and swatting her on the butt with a book and saying, "Move it, lardo."

Not that she was large—anything but. Jase just said that to everybody, all the time.

And everybody said equally nasty things back, of course. Everybody but Cheryl. All Cheryl did was turn bright red and stare at him with those pathetic eyes. It was like saying, "Do it again, Jase. I love to be tortured." The girl needed a full-time security officer.

And yet here she was in my dream, and now she really was a lardo. A great big one. It didn't make any sense.

I hadn't even seen Cheryl for a while. She'd disappeared. It had been at least two months since the principal had come on the P.A. and said that anyone who'd seen Cheryl, or knew anything about where she was, should let him know right away. Her parents hadn't seen her for a week.

And as far I knew, she hadn't been seen since. She certainly hadn't been back in school, and, like I said, I hadn't even thought about her—not until she suddenly strolled into my dream with a voice like a boom box and a face the size of your average prefab garden shed. Why?

I couldn't figure it out. And I couldn't stop thinking about it. The nightmare had upset me so much that I couldn't get back to sleep. As I lay there in the dark, my head filled with all sorts of strange, disconnected thoughts.

Or maybe not so disconnected. I found myself thinking about another girl who'd disappeared. It seemed that a lot of people were disappearing. A lot of kids, especially a lot of kids from my own neighborhood, Riverview.

This particular one I hardly knew at all, even though I'd saved her life once. It was last winter, back when things were weird, when I had all that trouble with the Strangers.

She was only five or six years old. She'd been playing all alone in Churchill Drive Park, down by the Monkey Paths, and she'd made the mistake of blowing on a horn she found there. The horn belonged to an especially nasty bunch of Strangers, a gang of them called the Sky Yelpers. It seems the favorite snack of these Yelper guys was raw human flesh—especially the flesh of humans who blew on that stupid horn.

So anyway, I managed to push the little girl out of the way of the Sky Yelpers and their very sharp teeth just in the nick of time, and got my hair badly mussed in the process. But was the kid grateful? No way. When the cops came, she told them I was trying to steal her horn.

Now she'd disappeared, too. And her entire house had gone along with her.

As I lay there thinking about it, I realized that it had happened about the same time Cheryl disappeared. A couple of months ago.

According to what I saw on the TV news, the little

girl's parents left her alone in the house for a half hour or so while they went up to Safeway to do some shopping. You'd think they'd know better than to leave a little kid alone like that, but they didn't. And while they were out, a storm came up. It was one of those really bad storms we sometimes get here in Winnipeg in the spring, with high winds and pounding rain and all. When that little girl's parents came out of Safeway and saw that storm, they finally remembered they were supposed to be parents and got a little worried about her, and they rushed home as fast as they could.

It was just a couple of blocks down Oakwood, but by the time they got there, the storm was over and the sun was out. Except for the huge puddles everywhere and the fallen tree branches lining the streets, you wouldn't even guess there'd been a violent storm raging just a few minutes earlier.

But there was one way that girl's parents could tell there had been a storm. Their house was gone. There was nothing left but a big hole in the ground. Their house was gone, and their daughter was gone with it.

She'd disappeared. Like Cheryl Zennor did a few months ago. Like a lot of kids seemed to be doing.

That kid hadn't been seen since, and neither had the house—which was the really strange part. The news guy on TV said that the high winds during the storm must have lifted it up off its foundation and carried it away. But if that was true, then where was it? Why hadn't it been found?

As I lay there in the dark, I suddenly remembered the address of that house. It was 313. 313 Oakwood. The TV guys really loved that—unlucky thirteen and all. Maybe that's why it stuck in my mind.

Well, it didn't make any sense, and I didn't like to think about it. Because if I did, there was just one obvious explanation—an explanation I didn't want to accept.

Them. The Strangers. Those nasty fairies who invaded the neighborhood last winter and caused all the trouble.

But it couldn't be them. Because the door between our country and theirs was closed. They couldn't come here anymore. That's what I'd been told, and the person who'd told me was an expert, a guy who'd studied all about the Strangers and who'd even spent some time in their country. So the door was closed, and they couldn't enter our world.

None of this was helping me get to sleep. How long would it be until morning finally came? How many more sleepless hours? I reached over to the night table, where my clock was. Reached over—and found myself touching something that wasn't supposed to be there.

It felt like a thick piece of cloth, and all ruffled. What the hell was that?

It seemed to be hanging in the air. And, as I groped around in the dark in an increasing panic, I realized it was all around me. It completely surrounded my bed, completely closed me in. Great, I thought. I'm being imprisoned by drapery. It's curtains for me.

Which meant I was still dreaming—dreaming about lying in my bed and being engulfed by a fiendish mass of fabric. I hate it when that happens, when you think you've woken up from a dream and then it just turns out that you're in a different dream. When that happens to you, even just once, how do you ever know again for certain that you've woken up? That you're ever really and truly awake and not just in another dream that hasn't ended yet?

I pinched myself on the arm really hard. I didn't wake up.

The dream wasn't going away. I groped around some more, trying to figure out what all that cloth was. And I found this opening in it.

I grabbed onto the opening and pulled it back to see where I was. Nothing. Pitch-black.

Then I stepped out of bed into the darkness—and fell flat on my face. The floor wasn't where I'd expected it to be. The bed seemed to be on some sort of platform. This was definitely not my bedroom. I had gone to sleep in my own bedroom, and somehow I'd woken up in a completely different place.

As I sat there rubbing my throbbing nose and cursing, I could see nothing but inky blackness. No luck. Finally my eyes adjusted enough to see that there was the slightest little glimmer of light coming from a spot over to my right.

I gingerly crept my way toward the glimmer, feeling in front of me with my hands, and carefully reached out toward it. More cloth.

But this time it sort of made sense. Cloth hanging over a glimmer of light. Curtains, I guessed—and this must be a window. I steeled myself, then grabbed hold and pulled the cloth aside.

Light flooded in, totally blinding me after all that darkness. It was a window, all right. A window filled with blinding light in the middle of the night. Why? I leaned forward, blinking at the strong light and sniffing what smelled like candle wax, and looked out. And after a bit, my eyes adjusted, and I could finally make sense of what I was seeing.

I was staring into an eyeball. A giant eyeball. Again.

TWO

The eyeball was so big that it completely filled the window frame. I couldn't even see its edges.

So, I thought, this is what a fly feels like when it navigates too close to a person's face. Small. Very small.

I told myself the eyeball was a figment of my imagination, just part of the dream. But it was a pretty big figment. And pretty repulsive, too. Why did my imagination have to be so accurate about putting in the red veins running through the white part? As I stared into my own reflection engulfed by the giant black pupil, I made a mental note to try to remember what I'd had for supper the night before, and to never have it again.

At which point, there was this thunderous noise. **"OOWAHOO WAHOO WAH OOWAH-NEE AHHH,"** it went. It was like being at a heavy metal concert. In the front row. The blast nearly knocked me over, and I staggered backward.

"OOPS!" the thunder said, a little less loudly. "IT'S MY VOICE, RIGHT?"

Voice? That loudness was somebody's voice? Not a bomb going off?

No. Just a voice to match the eye. The eye could talk. Or more accurately, bellow. I was dreaming about a bellowing eye. It had to be the sauerkraut. I told my mom I didn't like that sauerkraut, but would she listen?

"I'M WHISPERING NOW," the voice roared. "IS THAT BETTER?"

It was. I still found myself recoiling with each syllable, but now I could make out the words.

"Much better," I told the eyeball. "Thanks."

"HUH?" it boomed, moving even closer to the window. "WHAT WAS THAT? I CAN'T HEAR YOU."

Oh, great. A deaf eye. It sort of made sense. I mean, where would its ears be?

"MUCH BETTER!" I screamed at the top of my voice. Loud enough to make it blink, I guess, because a gigantic set of eyelashes quickly passed over the eyeball and then up again.

So the eyeball had a lid, too. How lifelike. There were even bits of that waxy yellow stuff caught in the lashes, like you get when you wake up from a long sleep—only these bits were the size of baseballs.

"IT'S YOU," the eyeball boomed. "I THOUGHT IT WAS. IT'S JOHNNY NESBIT, RIGHT?"

I wasn't surprised that the eyeball knew my name. It

was my nightmare, after all.

"BUT WHY," it added, **"ARE YOU SO SMALL?"**

This was a whole new twist. This was my nightmare—what was it doing asking questions about me? But hey—it was my mind inventing all this, right? And you've got to trust your own mind, or who can you trust? I might as well play along.

"I'M NOT SMALL," I shrieked at the eyeball. **"YOU'RE THE ONE THAT'S LARGE. AND AS FOR WHY . . ."**

I stopped and thought about it. I thought about it out loud. Why not out loud? There wasn't anybody there but me and my fantasy life.

"It beats me," I mused. "I'm just dreaming all this. I don't have to understand it, too. Maybe you represent my deep, hidden, inner anxiety about these zits I've been developing on my chin lately." I could see them reflected in the pupil, which is probably why I thought of them. "Yeah, I feel that people are staring at me all the time, and it makes me feel small. Maybe that's it. Maybe that's why I'm imagining you so big!"

The eyeball just kept right on staring at me.

"WHAT'S THAT?" it boomed. **"SORRY, BUT I CAN'T HEAR YOU. YOU'LL HAVE TO TALK LOUDER."**

"NEVER MIND!" I said.

"WHAT?" Then it paused for a moment, still staring intently at me. **"OH, THIS IS RIDICULOUS,"** it thundered. **"HOLD ON JUST A MINUTE!"**

The eyeball suddenly disappeared, and a blinding flash of orange filled the window. Then I heard the voice again. It was even louder than before.

"THERE!" it shrieked. **"THAT'S BET-TER!"**

By the time I stopped feeling the unbelievable pain and managed to get my own eyes unsquinched, the eyeball was filling up the window again.

"SAY SOMETHING!" it screamed. **"ANY-THING! I BET I CAN HEAR YOU NOW!"**

"AND I CAN HEAR YOU!" I shouted back. **"BOY, CAN I HEAR YOU! IF YOU DON'T LIGHTEN UP A LITTLE, YOU'RE GOING TO BREAK MY EARDRUMS!"**

"OH!" it shouted. **"SORRY. I *AM* WHISPERING, YOU KNOW. I GUESS I'LL HAVE TO WHISPER EVEN SOFTER.** IS THIS BETTER?"

It was like three supersonic jets taking off all at once, but it was better. Three was better than a squadron.

"Yeah," I said, my hands still over my ears.

"GOOD," the eye said, still staring at me. "I THOUGHT TAKING THAT OFF WOULD HELP. SO TELL ME—HOW DID YOU GET HERE?"

"How did *I* get here? What about you? I'm just having a dream and minding my own business. You're the thing that represents my repressed fears or whatever. Boy, do you ever represent them. I have to admit it, you've scared the pants off me."

"I DON'T KNOW WHAT YOU'RE TALKING

ABOUT. YOU'RE NOT IMAGINING ANYTHING. IT'S REAL. I'M REAL. ALTHOUGH COME TO THINK OF IT,"—and damned if it didn't seem to be giggling, if you can imagine thunder giggling—"I GUESS THAT HAVING THE PANTS SCARED OFF YOU JUST MIGHT EXPLAIN *WHY* YOU HAVEN'T GOT ANY PANTS ON."

What? I looked down. The eyeball was right. No pants.

So I sleep in the buff, big deal. And I was sleeping, wasn't I? Asleep, and having a nightmare.

A real nightmare. I mean, someone staring at your zits is bad enough, but this— I didn't even want to begin to think about what repressed fears this might be all about. As I took my hands off my ears and put them over my crotch, I could feel myself turning deep red. All over. I scurried quickly back to the bed, reached through the curtains for a blanket, and rolled myself up in it. Better. Much better.

Even though it was a shocking-pink blanket with big pink ruffles around the edge. I must have looked like a Valentine Day gift. And meanwhile, the eyeball just stayed there at the window, watching the whole sorry thing.

"YES," it finally boomed, "I GUESS ALL THIS MIGHT SEEM A LITTLE STRANGE TO YOU."

A *little* strange. Yeah, right, like nuclear warfare is a *little* dangerous.

"BUT," it went on," IT *IS* ALL REAL. I'M REAL. I

PROMISE YOU. YOU'RE WIDE AWAKE. AND SO AM I."

"YEAH, SURE," I shouted from where I was standing by the bed. "GIANT TALKING EYEBALLS ARE ALWAYS SHOWING UP OUTSIDE OF PEOPLE'S BEDROOM WINDOWS, RIGHT?"

"GIANT EYEBALLS? I'M NOT ANY GIANT EYEBALL."

"YOU SURE LOOK LIKE ONE TO ME."

"I DO? WAIT A MINUTE. I'LL STAND FARTHER BACK, SO YOU CAN SEE ALL OF ME."

The eyeball seemed to get smaller, and then it totally disappeared, leaving just a square of light. Then I could hear the voice, not quite so loud now, coming from some distance away.

"Okay," it said, sounding hardly like thunder at all. "I'm over on the other side of the room. Come to the window and take a look."

I did. I put my head out that window and looked. Up. Way, way up.

There was more of it, all right. A second giant eyeball next to the first one, and a giant nose right under them. Giant lips on a giant face. And a giant body underneath it all, holding a giant candle to light itself.

A giant body that looked a lot like a human being.

A giant body in an orange T-shirt and blue jeans.

A giant body that belonged to—

Cheryl Zennor.

Her again. I wake up from one nightmare about her

giant face and I end up in another nightmare about her being a giant all over. This time she was about three stories high. Her giant cheeks were blushing and her giant mouth was giving me this smile that would have seemed sort of gentle and pleasant, if it hadn't been about the size of a small automobile.

Even her eyes looked pleasant. From this distance, in fact, that giant eyeball I'd been so scared of just looked shy.

Hugely shy. Shy in the large economy size. For sure the nightmare was not over yet. I pinched myself again. Nothing happened. I was stuck in the nightmare.

Well, what could I do? I decided I might as well accept the fact that my life had turned into a nightmare and just get on with it. First things first, though. I had to find out why Cheryl was so huge.

But in order to do that I had to have a little chat with her—and that wasn't going to be easy. The size of her chat was making my ears hurt. The only thing I could think of was to tear a strip of ruffles off one of those curtains and wrap it around my head seven or eight times, like a sort of headband. I hoped it would muffle the noise a little.

So there I was, my head wrapped in a pink ruffle and a pink ruffled blanket wrapped firmly around me. If Cheryl said anything about it, I'd pound her one.

Yeah, sure. I'd pound her so hard she'd think a gnat had landed on her.

She was back at the window. I couldn't see anything

but that huge brown eye of hers, with the realistic red veins and all.

"A headband!" she boomed, but this time, the boom was sort of bearable—only a dull roar. "What a good idea! And it looks so sweet on your cute little head!" And then I could hear this insane loud cackle. She was laughing.

I quickly changed the subject. "So tell me, Ms. Giant. If you're not just a figment of my imagination, how come you're so enormous? Was it a special vitamin diet, or what?"

"Me, a giant? Don't be silly, Johnny. It's just me, Cheryl Zennor—Cheryl, you know, from your class at Churchill?"

I nodded.

"I'm just my usual normal size," she said. "You're the one that got small."

Not only was she huge, she had gone mad.

"Yeah, sure," I shouted. "Me and the entire world. Me and this stupid bedroom and blankets and sheets all got small, all at the very same time, and meanwhile, you were lucky enough to be the only thing in the entire universe to stay the same size."

"But Johnny, it's true. You're the small one. Except for that dollhouse you're in, everything else is my size."

"Dollhouse?" What was she talking about?

"Look," she said, "I'll show you."

The eye was gone, replaced by a giant red thing. It was an apple, a half-eaten apple the size of a weather balloon. And it had a wormhole in it that I could easily have crawled into, and I couldn't stop myself from thinking about the worm that had made it. Disgusting.

"See," she said, "this apple is big enough to feed you for a couple of months. You're tiny, Johnny, very, very tiny."

"Okay," I said, "I get the point. You think you haven't changed, and I *know* I haven't changed. So we're both the same as we've always been, and everything's hunky-dory, except that one of us is a giant and the other's the size of a bug. It only proves my point. This is a nightmare. I have to wake up."

"It's *not* a nightmare," she said, settling down on the floor some distance away from the window and dropping the apple into the fanny pack she was wearing around her waist. "I'm awake, and I'm real. I'm not in any nightmare."

"So where do you think you are, then? Where are you, and where am I? And most of all, how did we get here?"

"Well," she said, "I don't know about you . . ." She paused for a moment as a guilty look passed over her face. I could tell she knew more than she was willing to admit. "But as for me," she continued, "well, I know exactly how I got here."

"So how, then?"

"It's a long story," she said.

Three

What Cheryl told me did not make me happy.

It started when she was in Churchill Drive Park one day. Well, not in the park exactly, but in the woods down behind the hospitals, past the end of the park. Those woods join right onto the park, but they're not officially a part of it. That's why it's so wild down there. Nobody ever mows the grass or picks up all the garbage that people dump there. It's a desolate sort of place.

Cheryl went in the middle of the afternoon, on a school day. She was having a bad day at school, and she just had to get out. I could understand that, all right. What day wasn't a bad day at good old École Churchill? But she surprised me when she said, a little sheepishly, "It was your fault."

"My fault?" I said.

"You don't even remember, do you?"

I had to admit I didn't. Like I said, I hardly knew Cheryl. She was just this girl in my class. But after she told me, I remembered. It was, I suddenly realized, the last time I'd seen her, until now. And it was an embarrassing experience. Maybe that's why I'd managed to make myself forget it.

I was standing out in the hall, just by the door of my math class. I was minding my own business, waiting for the other class to come out of the room. Cheryl was standing there beside me, waiting, too—not that I really noticed her, not until it was too late. She was so shy that if you even smiled at her a little she just blushed and looked down at her shoes. So I guess I'd learned not to look at her. Anyway, the bell rang, and everyone in the other class rushed out all at once, and one of them must have pushed into Cheryl, because she began to topple forward, right into me.

I reached out to grab her without even thinking about it. And there she was, in my arms, her body pressed up against mine, staring up into my eyes. It was the first time I'd ever held a girl.

The look on her face was, well, strange. Not unhappy or frightened, just . . . strange. And, like I said, embarrassing. It kind of froze me—I couldn't let go and I couldn't stop staring at her.

At which point, Jason Garrett strolled by and said "Hey, Nesbit, I knew you were a stud, man—but during school hours?" And then he started doing that horse snorting he calls a laugh.

Cheryl turned bright red. So did I, I guess. Then she pulled herself away from me and bolted off down the hall. Which was just what I felt like doing. No wonder I'd blotted it out of my memory.

Anyway, Cheryl told me, after all that happened, she had gone out the back door and headed off down the road toward the park without even thinking about where she was going. It wasn't just because of me, she said—that was just the last straw. She didn't tell me about the other straws. And she was walking in the woods when she heard a whining sound, like somebody crying. She thought maybe some little kid had gotten lost or something, so she went to investigate, to a little hollow off the path and close to the riverbank. It wasn't a kid. It was a dog, a scruffy-looking brown-and-white dog.

When it saw Cheryl, it got on his feet and started growling at her. And instead of acting like a sensible person and hightailing it out of there, she started talking to it. It was its eyes, she told me. They had tears in them— as if dogs could cry. But she thought she saw tears, and so she decided the growling was just a big act. And it turned out she was right. She ended up sitting there with that dog, rubbing its fur and comforting it, for hours.

But then, suddenly, the dog got tense and started growling again. Cheryl could tell he was frightened of something, but there was nothing there—nothing she could see, at least. Then the dog leapt to its feet and started to run in circles around her, yelping away as if it'd been burned or something. And then it just took off.

Almost literally took off, Cheryl said. One moment it was there circling around her and the next it was gone— and, she told me, she could almost have sworn its feet weren't even touching the ground.

The dog taking off like that made Cheryl feel even worse than before. Real bad. So bad, she started to cry. She couldn't hold it back.

I don't know why she told me all that. It was facts I was after, just facts. I didn't need to know about her feelings. I didn't *want* to know about her feelings, especially after that business in the hall. And anyway, Cheryl wasn't the kind of person I ever expected to tell me about her feelings. But I think it was my size that did it. Me being so small, I must have seemed like a little doll to her—a toy she could play with. She didn't have to be shy around a toy. She could say whatever she wanted.

I just wished she didn't want to be so honest.

Anyway, she said, she was sobbing away to beat the band and this guy showed up—an older guy, sort of middle-aged. He must have been moving real quietly, because she didn't even know he was there until she suddenly felt his hand on her shoulder and heard a voice saying, "There, there, it can't be that bad, can it?"

She thought about running away. He was a stranger, right? And you're not supposed to talk to strangers. But for some reason, she didn't run away. For a while she just cried, and he just watched. Then, finally, he put his arm around her.

She bolts down the hall when harmless little me tries

to save her from a bad fall, and she lets this guy put his mitts on her for no reason at all in the middle of a lonely forest. He must have hypnotized her or something. Either that, or I have about as much sex appeal as a wombat.

Anyway, he held her for a while, until she stopped crying. And then he got her to tell him what was wrong, and she did. Every straw of it.

And according to her, it was wonderful. He understood everything. He knew exactly how she felt. The look on her face when she told me that was enough to make you barf. It was like when Dorothy says "there's no place like home" in *The Wizard of Oz*.

Anyway, he was so totally gosh-awful wonderful that she told him all about herself and her life and her problems and probably even her shoe size. And then he said good-bye and left. And she followed him.

That's right. Followed him, just like some dumb little homeless kitten. He headed off down the path and through the park, and she just crept along behind him. Either Cheryl was crazier than I thought, or she was under a spell. I voted for the spell.

As she walked, it gradually stopped being the park. I know that doesn't make much sense, but that's what she told me. There started to be too many trees. You could hardly see the river through them, and then you couldn't see the river at all. And the leaves were so lush they made everything seem green, she said. Everything, even the bits of sky she could see coming through the leaves.

Finally, the creepy old pervert stopped and looked at her, and said, "What? Still there?" and he gave her this large frown. Cheryl just stood there and hoped he wasn't going to send her away.

"Well, then," he said, and smiled at her. "I guess we'll have to keep you, won't we?"

And he did. He kept her.

He kidnapped her. Not that *she* saw it like that, of course.

"Oh, Johnny," she told me, her huge face glowing, "I just couldn't believe it! He wanted me. He actually wanted *me*, Cheryl Zennor!"

They walked the rest of the way side by side. The path got twistier and twistier and finally led to a gate in a high wall that went off into the forest in both directions. They went through the gate into a garden, and in the middle of the garden was a house.

"An adorable house, Johnny, with stone walls and sweet little bay windows!" She gestured excitedly around the room as she talked about it. "*His* house! This house! And I've been here ever since."

"So," I said, wishing it wasn't true, "that's where we are, then. In that pervert's house?"

"Yes. *His* house. My master's. And he isn't a pervert, Johnny. He's wonderful! He has all these wonderful children here, you know, and—"

"Children?"

"Yes, children, a whole bunch. And they're all just such sweet loveable kids. I look after them. I'm the nanny here! I wake them up in the morning and get them dressed and make sure they eat their breakfast, and I play with them all day, and I give them their baths and everything!"

She was so excited her giant eyes were sparkling. All because some old pervert was treating her like a slave.

Well, if she wanted to play Mary Poppins, let her. Let her feed and clothe and give baths to as many little monsters as she wanted. Let her achieve a state of perfect bliss, surrounded by twenty thousand screaming brats all needing their diapers changed and their backs burped at the same time. It was her business, not mine.

My business was getting my butt out of this whole ridiculous situation. Because I didn't like it. I didn't like it at all. It was very suspicious, and I was beginning to know who to be suspicious of—a certain bunch of creatures whose name begins with *S* and ends with *trangers*. It had all their earmarks.

The first thing to do was get out of this stupid bedroom or whatever it was and case the joint. But how? For one wild moment I thought about climbing out the window—a pretty dumb thought, because I could see I was way up off the ground—probably on the second floor of whatever building I was in.

Then I realized I didn't have to climb out the window. I was in a bedroom, and a bedroom was likely to be part of a house, and a house had to have a door. I could find that door, walk through it, and see what was going on out there.

I turned around to take a closer look at the room I was standing in. The candle was throwing just enough light through the window for me to make things out.

The bed was a four-poster with a canopy over the top, a frilly pink canopy with pink curtains covered with rows and rows of ruffles. And, as I'd discovered so painfully before, the bed was standing on a platform, and the platform had pink ruffles all around it, too. The rest of the room was filled with ornately carved furniture, all in white, some of it also with pink cloth ruffles on it. And I could just barely make out the big pink flowers on the wallpaper.

Talk about your nightmares—I'd woken up in Barbie's Pretty in Pink Primping Parlor. One good thing, though. There was a door.

I went over and opened it, doing my best to ignore Cheryl's anxious voice, which was asking me where I was going and telling me to come back at once before something bad happened. What did she think I was, a china figurine or something?

It was dark on the other side of the door, but as I clutched the blanket more tightly around me and moved out into the darkness, I could see, somewhere down below me in the distance, a little glimmer of light. It had to be Cheryl's candle, shining through a window or something. I began to head toward it, feeling my way forward. I did a pretty good job of it, too. I managed to stop myself after I'd fallen down no more than three or four of the stairs of the staircase that turned out to be there right in front of me.

After I carefully made my way down the rest of the stairs one by one, I saw that the light was coming through a little window, and that the window was in a door. I was standing in the front hallway, and that door was the way out.

As I looked through the window in the door, I could see Cheryl's candle shining way up over my head and looking like a streetlight. Behind and above it, Cheryl's face was gleaming like the moon. I opened the door and went down the front steps and started to head over to her.

And suddenly I felt this force—this huge force—push against me and bowl me over backwards.

Right on my butt. I lay there on the ground in deep pain, carefully feeling the air in front of me, trying to figure out what had hit me.

I figured it out. It hadn't hit me—I had hit it. And it hadn't pushed me—it only felt like that. It was a wall. I was touching an invisible wall.

Four

Cheryl must have heard the noise I made when I crashed into the wall, because when I finally stopped wincing from the pain and opened my eyes, I could see her up there above me, on her hands and knees, peering down at me. Up this close, she looked really, really huge. I would have been frightened if I hadn't been so busy feeling intense pain.

"Poor little thing," she said. "Well, I did try to stop you. Are you okay?"

"I'm fine," I said angrily. "And I'd be grateful if you'd stop calling me a little thing, Ms. Jumbo. What's going on here, anyway? What did I bump into? It must be Stranger magic—some kind of force field, maybe?"

"A force field? Honestly, Johnny, you're just letting your imagination run away with you. It's just glass."

"Glass?" I touched it again. She was right.

"Yeah, glass. Didn't you know? You're inside a bottle—sort of like a family-size Pepsi bottle, except made of glass. You and the whole house you're in. If you look up over your head there, you'll be able to see the hole for the cork."

I looked. Sure enough, up high in the air, just visible past the edge of the roof of the house, was what looked like a round circle floating in the sky. A hole for a cork.

"Here's the cork, see?" She waved this object she was holding. It looked like—well, like a cork.

A huge cork. I was inside a bottle, like a bug in a science fair project. I could even imagine the name of the project: An Example of What Happens When You Bottle Up Your Anger.

Because I was feeling very angry. If I ever figured out how all this had happened to me and who had made it happen, I was going to strangle that person with my own two hands.

"I pulled the cork out before so I could hear you better," Cheryl added. "This isn't the only bottle, either. There must be about thirty others, just like this one. See?" She got her candle and held it up in the air.

They were there, all right, all around me. They did look sort of like Pepsi bottles, except each one had a building in it. They were really peculiar buildings, too—the kind you read about in fairy tales. Some looked like cottages with thatched roofs, and some looked like huge castles with towers and battlements.

I turned to look at the house behind me, the one I'd

just come out of, expecting to see another castle. But it was just an ordinary house, the kind of house you find all over Winnipeg. It was a two-story job in white stucco. As I stood there looking at it, something suddenly penetrated my brain.

The house number over the door. It was 313.

That house on Oakwood—the one that had disappeared during the storm with the little girl in it. It was 313, too.

In fact, it was this very house. Now that I was really looking at it, I recognized it. The green shutters, the wrought-iron railings on the little porch, the funny sort of circle patterns in the stucco. I'd passed by that house hundreds of times on my way home from Safeway.

I had gone to sleep in my own bedroom on Wavell Avenue and woken up in 313 Oakwood—seven blocks over.

But it wasn't seven blocks over now. 313 Oakwood was being kept inside a bottle in a strange giant house in the middle of a forest in Stranger country.

Because it had to be Stranger country. None of it made any sense. It was creepy.

"I don't get it," I said. "Just where are we, anyway? What is this place?"

"I . . . I'm not sure," Cheryl said hesitantly, looking up and glancing around the room. "It's some kind of storeroom, I think. I've never been in it before." She turned toward me. "See, what happened was, little Angie, she loves to play ball, and this afternoon out in the garden she lost her ball. We looked everywhere, but no luck. I was going to ask the master for a new ball for her, but somehow it slipped my mind when I saw him this evening. I get so rattled sometimes when he's around, I just can't think straight. Anyway, Angie couldn't sleep tonight because of the ball. She kept waking up and crying. And I know the master always comes in here when I ask him for stuff for the kids, so, well, I . . . just came in here myself."

So she'd been sneaking around in the dark behind the old guy's back.

"That's how I found you," she said. "The thing is, after I came through the door I couldn't believe how big this place was. From the way things look outside the house, it ought to be just a tiny closet. But it isn't. So . . . I started to look around. There's all this strange stuff in here, Johnny. So I was looking at it all, and I picked up this thing, and it was a . . ." She paused then for a moment. "Well, never mind what it was. It's not important, because that's when I heard this noise. A scream, sort of. But a really tiny scream, coming from these glass bottles. So I came over, and that's when I saw there were houses and castles inside them. I knelt down and looked through the windows of some of them, and everything is so tiny, and it's all perfectly proportioned. And so realistic, too. I mean, some of them even have miniature dirty dishes on the tables and miniature clothes strewn around the bedroom floors. It's so sweet."

"Yeah, sure," I said. "Sweet. Just like me."

"But I do think you're—I mean *they're* . . ." By this time she looked very confused, and her face was bright red all over again. "Oh," she wailed, "why am I telling you this?"

Then she gulped and went on all in a rush. "Anyway, the noise was coming from inside *this* house, the normal one—so I looked through the window—and there *you* were." She gave me this weird intense look and then, for no reason at all, she blushed again.

Well, no time to worry about it. I had to get out of that bottle. Now that I knew I was in it, I hated being there. I felt, well, all bottled up.

I looked up again. That hole was pretty high up over my head, but there had to be some way for me to get up there. If I could get up onto the roof somehow, through a second-floor window or something, and . . . well, maybe then I could get Cheryl to reach in and . . .

I didn't even want to begin thinking about that part. I mean, I'd never even been close to a girl, except that time in the hall with Cheryl, and now this. It wasn't the kind of thing they ever got around to covering in Family Life class.

As it happened, however, I didn't need to think about it. Because by now I could see that Cheryl had finished her blushing and was busily rooting through that pack she had on around her waist.

"I thought I had this in here," she finally said. Her hand came out of the pack holding a white shoelace. "I like to keep some handy," she added, "because you never know when a kid's going to need one. Like right now."

I had to hand it to her. It was a great idea. Of course, it would have been even better if the shoelace had been longer—like, long enough to reach down to me on the floor of the bottle. I had to go back into the house and up the stairs and through the bedroom, and then out the window onto the little porch over the front door.

But after I got onto the porch roof, it was easy. What Cheryl called a shoelace was like a clothesline rope to me. I just tied the end of it around my waist and around the blanket, of course—I wasn't going anywhere without that blanket. Then I told Cheryl to haul away, and up I went.

And out. Freedom!

Freedom and nausea. Cheryl decided to have a closer look at me, and she pulled me up toward her face so quickly that I started to swing back and forth on the shoelace. Back and forth, back and forth, and every back made my feet higher than my head, and every forth brought me almost right up to that gigantic mouth of hers, and she was smiling so gigantically as she looked at me that I could see right down past those gleaming giant teeth into the dark cavern of her throat. I didn't know whether it was the swinging or the mouth that was making my stomach churn. Maybe it was just the goopy expression on Cheryl's face, which clearly showed just how cute and adorable she was finding me.

"Put me down!" I shouted on a swing away from Cheryl's face. "Right now."

She did, so fast my stomach made an even larger flip.

I sat myself down and waited for it to settle. Then I looked up at Cheryl. From this close range she was truly monstrous. It was like looking at someone through a magnifying glass. Ordinarily I wouldn't even have noticed the little zits she had on her chin, but now each one was about the size of my whole head. And as for the smell of her sneakers—well, I guess it was just normal sneaker smell, but it's hard to think of it as normal when it's been magnified about fifty times. I waited for my stomach to settle once more.

As I waited, I took a look back at the bottle, and something caught my eye, up high around the back of the house. It was a label, and there were words on it, but from down below I couldn't make out what they were.

"Cheryl," I said. "That label up there. What does it say?"

"Ah yes, the label. I . . . I think maybe it isn't a good idea to read it out loud. You'd better go up and see for yourself."

Which is how I found myself in midair beside Cheryl's huge face, standing in the middle of a large pinkish bumpy surface, trying not to think about what the surface actually was or who it was attached to, while I moved my weight from one foot to the other to keep my balance as I read the words.

I don't know what I expected. "May contain human

matter," perhaps. Or "Caution: Contents under great pressure and may explode at any moment."

But what I read was something completely different. It was a poem. Written in funny old-fashioned letters:

> Preserved inside are human things
> Reduced in size; but he who brings
> The strength of mind and force of fist
> To take the cork and twist the wrist,
> He soon will see, before his eyes
> Them all become their proper size.
> Just take the cork and wave it high
> And say the words you here descry;
> Then things will come from out the bottle—
> First few will grow, and then a lot'll.
> So say the words that do the deed—
> The words are, "Make It Grow With Speed!"

For a while after reading that, I just stood there balancing on that wavery flesh-colored floor for a while and felt sad. The words on that label meant one thing for sure. Cheryl was right after all. "Human things reduced in size." It was me who was small and not her that was large.

Yeah, I'd actually turned into a miniature action figure, a cute little dolly-wolly. I was adorable, like she said. I was standing on her hand. I was even wearing a pink blanket with ruffles on it, for cripes' sake. The word "humiliating" hardly even begins to cover it.

But I didn't have to keep on being humiliated. Not according to that label up there.

"That's it!" I said. "Hand me that cork!" I wasn't exactly sure how I was going to wave it high when it was about twice as tall as me and three times as wide. But if that was the way to get back to my normal size again, then I was going to do it somehow. If that's what it took, I would wave a grand piano.

"DO YOU THINK THAT'S REALLY A GOOD IDEA?" Cheryl said. At this range, her voice sounded like grand opera, even through my ruffled earmuffs.

As I winced, I steamed. Was she planning to keep me for a toy and play house with me all day?

"A good idea?" I shrieked. "Of course it's a good idea. Do it. Now."

Her face looked really worried. I took a step back. If my hand happened to get caught in one of the furrows in her forehead, it would disappear up to the elbow.

"BUT, JOHNNY," she said. **"WHAT IF . . . WELL, IF IT WORKS, AND _EVERYTHING_ IN THAT BOTTLE GROWS TO ITS RIGHT SIZE. . . ."**

As she said it, I could imagine it happening. Not just me returning to my right size, but the house, too. The house expanding, the walls moving out, the glass shattering, everything getting bigger, bigger. . . .

If the house grew to its right size, it would be higher than the room it was in now. It would probably send the roof of this place flying and make the whole cottage tumble down. I'd be my normal size, all right—with a roof about to crush me to death.

Cheryl could see I'd figured it out. **"THAT'S WHY I DIDN'T WANT TO SAY THOSE WORDS ALOUD BEFORE,"** she said. **"WHY I WANTED YOU TO READ THE POEM YOURSELF."**

A dummy like me would have just read those words and waved that cork without even thinking about it. But Cheryl had been thinking about it. I began to develop some respect for her.

A thought occurred to me. "Hey, I know," I said. "You could cart the bottle outside, and *then* we'd say the words."

"But where outside? Not in the garden. If we grow the house there, the master will know I've been in here, fooling around with his stuff."

True. "Well, in the woods, then. You said there were woods surrounding this place, right? So we take the bottle into the woods, away from the cottage."

"No, Johnny, it can't be done. The woods are so thick, once you get past the edge of the garden you can't even walk between the trees. That's why we couldn't find Angie's ball. It's like a solid wall. Even the path I walked in on has grown together again."

Magic, probably. She was a prisoner here, and she didn't even know it.

Well, there had to be some way out of this mess. I just couldn't think of what exactly it was yet. I would figure it out eventually, I told myself, as I stood there wavering on Cheryl's hand in a state of deep depression. But for now I was stuck. For now and the near future at least, I was a doll-sized person wearing a stupid pink blanket and being shouted at by a giant.

Once I got myself out of this mess and back to normal, I told myself, I would never complain about my life ever again. Never.

Well, except for Language Arts maybe.

Five

Cheryl told me she had to get back to the children. It was almost morning, and they'd be waking up. And until we figured out what to do about my predicament, there didn't seem to be anything sensible for me to do but to get back inside the bottle. At least everything in there was my size.

So I wrapped the shoelace around my middle again, and Cheryl lifted me up and dropped me down onto the porch roof of the house again. Then she promised she'd come back in a few hours with some food for me and reeled up the lace and stuck the cork back in the bottle—just in case that master of hers happened to come in and notice something was wrong, she said. Then she took off. And took the candle with her, of course, and left me standing on that roof alone in darkness.

Total darkness. So I considered myself lucky that I only

almost fell off the roof, and that I only banged my arm into the window frame *once* while getting back into the house.

And then I waited.

I waited for a long time. It seemed like an eternity. I mean, what could I do? It was too dark to see anything. There was nothing to do but sit on that stupid bed and fume about how totally powerless I felt.

So I sat, and I fumed. And I fumed, and I sat. And the time passed. And Cheryl didn't come back.

At first I told myself it just *seemed* like a long time, that I was so totally bored that it just felt like forever and that she'd be there any minute. Then I started to panic. What if she *never* came back? What if I was stuck inside the bottle forever? I'd die of starvation. Before that, I'd die of boredom.

For a while I considered tackling the stairs, even in the pitch black. There had to be a kitchen down there somewhere. Sure, all the stuff in the fridge would be spoiled after all this time—but maybe there'd be, like, Cheerios or something in the cupboard? I could survive on Cheerios. And at least I'd be doing something.

But I kept putting it off, because, hey, she could come back at any minute, and I wasn't really all that hungry.

And it was *so* dark.

And then I headed off into the dark anyway. I had to. I needed to pee. Yeah, there I was, tiny and bottled up and in the middle of weird happenings and scared of the dark, and I still had to pee so bad that I was desperate. Isn't nature wonderful?

I did manage to find the bathroom, finally, after a few unexpected meetings with walls and chairs and stuff. But I can't guarantee that all the pee actually went into the toilet. It's hard to aim in the dark.

Then I made my way back to the bed and sat down and told myself to be calm. Cheryl wouldn't just leave me here to starve. Unless, of course, there'd been a nuclear holocaust or something out there, and she couldn't come back because she had a broken arm or leg or maybe her head was blown entirely off. Or maybe that master of hers had found her trying to sneak back in there and got mad at her and changed her into a frog.

It would serve her right for deserting me like this. I started to imagine Cheryl with slimy green skin and big frog eyes—and then, suddenly, there she was, at the bedroom window, Cheryl with her giant green warts glinting and her loud voice croaking.

And then things got really confusing—I think it was something about how Cheryl was going to kiss me and change *me* into a frog, too, but I'm not really sure. I must have been hallucinating, I guess. I'd been in there for so long by then that I'd probably used up most of the oxygen in the bottle. So much for Cheryl's bright idea of putting the cork back in.

Anyway, the next thing that made any sense was a voice, which at first seemed to be coming from a giant eye with a froggy-type mouth where the iris should be. "JOHNNY," it shouted, "ARE YOU THERE? ARE YOU OKAY?" And I shook my head, and the eye disappeared, and I could breathe again.

"Wha . . . what happened?" I said.

"OH, THANK GOODNESS," the voice bellowed. "YOU'RE ALIVE."

It was Cheryl, at the window—still a giant, alas, but no frog.

"Where *were* you, anyway?" I demanded angrily, after I'd climbed out the window and she'd fished me out of the bottle again and dropped me to the floor. "I could have died in there. And I'm starving!"

"I know, Johnny," she said. "But I couldn't help it. I did bring some food. See?" She reached into that pack of hers and brought out a slice of pizza wrapped in a napkin, which she put down on the floor in front of me on top of the napkin. To me it looked like a living-room carpet with a particularly fancy design—pepperoni slices the size of, well, pizzas. But if I had to eat a carpet, I had to eat a carpet. I was too hungry to care much about what the food looked like.

Or about manners. I just got down on my knees in front of the carpet of pizza and grabbed a slice of pepperoni and started nibbling away at its edges as tomato sauce dribbled down my arm.

As I gnawed my way around the edge of that pepperoni slice, Cheryl told me what had happened. She had come back just as she said she would, sometime in the middle of the morning. That was when her boss always seemed to disappear from sight for an hour or two, and she figured it would be safe. She'd left those kids out playing in the garden and snuck back into the house and opened the door to this room. And behind the door was—a closet.

"Just a little broom closet," she said, "like I thought there would be in the first place."

So how do you get back into a room when the room isn't there anymore? Cheryl told me she tried everything she could think of. She closed the closet door and opened it again two or three times. No luck. Then she went into the closet and felt all along the walls and floor, hoping there was maybe some kind of secret knob or handle or something that would open up into the room she'd been in the night before. No luck. Then she banged on the walls, trying not to be too noisy and hoping to maybe break through. No luck. Finally, she had to get back to the kids. But she came back three more times, and each time it was still just a broom closet. By then, she said, she was starting to panic.

"Because the most obvious explanation," she said, "was that he knew. The master, I mean. He knew I'd been in here, and he'd closed it off somehow so I couldn't get back in again. And that meant he knew I was sneaking behind his back. He'd make me leave. Oh, Johnny," she wailed, "I don't want to leave. I love it here."

But she kept on trying. She knew she was taking a chance, had maybe already ruined everything for herself for that master guy. But she kept on trying anyway, because of me.

And I know I ought to have been grateful about that.

But for some reason all I did was feel angry. I guess I just didn't like having my fate in somebody else's hands like that. It made me feel so . . . so little.

To cover my feelings, I walked around the pizza to the other side, then got down on my knees and reached over for a nice-looking hunk of olive that was just a teensy bit beyond my reach, but if I put my right hand down, I could balance on it and reach the olive with my other hand, and . . .

"Is this what you want?" Just as I'd finished sinking my right hand up to the wrist in tomato sauce, Cheryl had reached down, picked up the piece of olive between her thumb and her first finger, and stuck it in front of my face.

"Not anymore," I said coldly, getting to my feet and giving her a nasty look as I shook my right hand vigorously and sauce flew in all directions. "Tell me the rest."

Cheryl just looked at me for a moment. Then she shook her head a little.

"Tsk, tsk," she said. It was under her breath, but it was still loud enough for me to hear, it being a giant's breath and all. Then she stuck *my* piece of olive into her mouth and gulped it down in one bite, and then told me the rest as I stood there licking the sauce off my hand and tried not to feel furious with her.

After the afternoon had passed and dinner was over and all the kids were finally asleep, Cheryl decided to give it one more try. And this time, when she opened the door, the closet was gone and this room was here. Finally.

Maybe it was only here at night? Or only at certain moments?

She didn't stop to think about why. She'd rushed in, shouted at me, got no response, removed the cork, still got no response.

"Then I got really frightened," she said. "I was just about ready to try anything. Pick the bottle up and give it a good shake. Maybe turn it over and tip you out. Anything to get you out of there."

I was horrified. "Tip the bottle?" I said. "Shake it? It didn't occur to you that all that heavy furniture would be on top of me?"

"I really wasn't thinking, Johnny. I was frantic. And anyway, I didn't have to. Because that's when you woke up."

"How lucky for me," I said, licking the last remains of the tomato sauce off my hand. "This pizza is very salty. Do you have anything to drink?"

She had an apple juice box in her pack. But even with lots of stretching and gaping I could just barely get my mouth around the straw—and then I couldn't produce enough suction to pull up any apple juice.

"I could maybe pour some juice into the palm of my hand," Cheryl offered, "and you could lap it up."

"What do you think I am, a kitten? No way."

I finally agreed to let her pour some onto the napkin. Then I picked up the corner of the napkin, put it in my mouth, and sucked out the juice. You can't begin to imagine how delicious it tasted. An impertinent young juice with just a haunting suspicion of Kleenex.

After I sucked down my drink, we talked a little about what to do next. One thing was clear—I couldn't stay in the bottle anymore, not if the door wasn't going to be a door to this room on any kind of consistent basis. What if Cheryl couldn't get back in here for a long time? Or ever? I'd starve to death. Or I'd die of terminal bruises received while heading for the toilet. Nope, she had to take me with her.

We decided I'd travel in that pack of hers—the one she wore around her waist.

"It's probably the best place for you to stay all the time," she said. "I always carry it with me, because I need all this stuff for the kids. So nobody would wonder why I had it. And then you'd always be with me, always safe."

I asked her to drop me into it on the shoelace so I could check it out. It was a jungle in there. In the murky gloom of the light cast by Cheryl's candle, I made my way down through pens, pencils, safety pins, Kleenexes, combs, brushes, thread, needles—I got a good jab from one of those needles. Toy cars and trucks, some hard candies in cellophane wrappers. A Phillips screwdriver, some screws, a whole bunch of Band-Aids, a bottle of baby aspirin. More Kleenex, this time used. Wonderful. And the whole place smelled like old snot and baby powder.

But I could tell it would be sort of cozy, once we got some of that junk out of there. I shouted at Cheryl to haul me up and agreed to her plan.

First, though, I made her drop me back into the giant

Pepsi bottle and then shine her candle through the windows as I did some exploring. Just because I was leaving the bottle didn't mean that I had to give up all the comforts of home. All that stuff in there was the right size for me, and I was about to go on a camping expedition for who knew how long, inside a foul-smelling fanny pack. I'd decided to help myself to some equipment.

In fact, as I rummaged through the kitchen, I was sorry I hadn't thought of it earlier. There were glasses in there—apple juice–size glasses. I finally settled on a plastic one I could cart along without worrying about breakage. I also found knives and forks that would be perfect for cutting up pizza-size pepperoni slices, and a couple of rolls of paper towels for dealing with leftover tomato sauce. And best of all for the fanny pack, a can of air freshener.

Elsewhere in the house, in various closets, I found me-sized versions of all kinds of things, including a knapsack and, best of all, a flashlight. No more stumbling around in the dark. No sleeping bag, though, so I was still stuck with the blanket. It was okay for sleeping, in the dark, when you couldn't see the ruffles.

Anyway, by the time she finally hauled me out of there, I had three garbage bags full of everything I might need.

Even toothpaste and a toothbrush. Actually, I hadn't thought of those myself—Cheryl made me go back and get them.

"And floss, too, Johnny. Don't forget the floss."

I had everything, all right, including a big pain in the butt. Very big. That was when I decided I needed to take some Tylenol, too.

I was especially grateful for the set of earplugs I found in the medicine chest beside the Tylenol bottle. I put them on and ditched my ruffled earmuff. They were terrific. Cheryl now sounded just like a normal human talking, except for going on about flossing.

So I had everything I needed. Everything, that is, except clothes, which was what I wanted most of all. But all the clothes closets in that house were filled with little girls' dresses covered with ruffles and bows and flowers. Pink mostly.

A closet in one of the other bedrooms upstairs did have some men's clothes in it, but they were all huge on me. The guy that lived there must have been about the size of a sumo wrestler. I'd need Cheryl's shoelace to keep up the pants, and I'd have to roll up the legs so much I wouldn't be able to put my knees together.

But I wasn't about to spend the rest of my life wearing nothing but that blanket, which looked even more disgusting with tomato stains all over it, so I talked Cheryl into uncorking a few more bottles and letting me drop in for a little visit. The castles were a disappointment. There were clothes in them, all right, but they were things like tights and doublets and frilly collars. I'd rather wear a blanket, thank you. But in one of the cottages, I struck gold—a closet with some work pants and work shirts just about my size. The material was kind of rough and scratchy, and they smelled even worse than Cheryl's sneakers. But I helped myself to three or four changes, anyway, including socks and some strange-looking long underwear with convenient openings both in front and in back. There was even a pair of very muddy boots. This stuff was going to make me look like a fugitive from a farmer's convention. But who was going to see me in it, anyway?

The one thing I didn't see in any of those houses was people. All that human clothing and furniture and stuff, and no humans. It was creepy, kind of. How come I was the only person in the entire bottle village?

After I'd finished my search, Cheryl recorked all the bottles and dropped me down into her fanny pack along with all my new possessions. I changed into one of the new outfits (first telling Cheryl to zip up the pack—I could do without her looking at me with those big goopy eyes of hers and now, thank goodness, I had my flashlight).

Once the undies were on, I felt much better. Fully clothed, I sighed a sigh of relief. Then I snuggled down on top of my pink blanket, carefully spread out over the garbage bag full of clothes to protect me from all the sharp objects below, and shouted to Cheryl to get moving. And with a bit of a lurch, I headed off for a new life in the big world outside my bottle.

Six

Traveling in a fanny pack is not exactly the last word in luxury. It's more or less okay if your means of locomotion—the person wearing the pack, that is—just keeps walking on a level. Then it's only regular jolts and jumps, like being on a boat in choppy waves on a very windy day. You feel sort of queasy, but at least it's steady and you know what to expect. You get into the rhythm of it—like regularly being hit on the head with a hammer.

But if the means of locomotion decides to bend over or come to a sudden stop or something like that, then everything suddenly rolls over to one side and hits you on the head. It hurts.

We finally came to a halt in the big dorm where Cheryl slept with all those kids. Or so she said—I didn't actually get to see it. I didn't actually see anything until some hours later, when Cheryl finally let me out of the pack.

In the meantime, there was a sort of major earthquake as Cheryl undid the pack and took it off. She *did* warn me before she did it, but that doesn't help much when you've bounced off a little metal car the size of yourself and ended up with your nose and the rest of your face engulfed by a crumpled-up Kleenex the size of a basketball.

After that, though, there was peace and quiet. Cheryl put the pack down—beside her on the bed, she said, so she could hear me if I needed anything in the night—and told me to get some sleep. And I did. I was asleep almost as soon as I got the earplugs out and climbed under the blanket.

Cheryl slept, too—really soundly. At one point I was awakened by a noise like a giant saw buzzing away at logs in Paul Bunyan's lumber mill. Cheryl snoring. I put the earplugs in again. Now it just sounded like a couple of helicopters landing. And taking off and landing again and again and again, until it turned into a dream about helicopters with giant eyes and frog flippers.

The next thing I knew, I was in another earthquake. Cheryl was putting the pack back on—very carefully, or so she claimed. Those little metal car manufacturers really need to do something about those sharp edges.

It was morning. Cheryl was awfully busy, getting all those kids dressed and their teeth brushed and making sure they ate their breakfast. I made it through all her moving around and bending with only one or two minor mishaps. One of them involved Cheryl's tweezers and a part of my anatomy that shall remain unnamed. I jumped about a foot.

"Okay, Johnny," I finally heard her say. "It's safe now for a few moments. You can come out." And the roof over my head unzipped, and there was a burst of light and then Cheryl's giant eyes staring down at me.

"Jeez," I said as I adjusted to the light. "It's about time. Get me out of here. And quick." I guess I'd sucked up way too much apple juice because of that salty pizza. I was desperate again.

As I said "Hurry hurry hurry hurry hurry," Cheryl fished out the end of the shoelace, which I'd already tied around my waist in anticipation of her arrival, and dropped me to the ground. I found myself in a thick jungle of narrow green trees. Grass.

"Turn your head," I shouted as I fumbled desperately with the buttons of my fly. "Right now."

She did, and I watered the grass, for a long time. Blessed relief.

After I buttoned up and told Cheryl she could look again, she pulled me up to where she was sitting and put me down beside her.

It was a sort of stone surface, like a curving road heading off into the distance. Or more like a bridge, because it suddenly came to an end a short distance away on both sides of me, and past that I could see nothing but air on both sides.

"Where are we?" I asked.

"Out in the garden. We're sitting on the well."

I walked over to one of the edges, leaned out, and looked down. There was the lawn I'd just been maintaining, about four stories below. Scary. I edged myself back, then trotted over to the other side. This time there was a lake below me, a perfectly round lake surrounded by huge stone walls. A very deep-looking lake, dark, mysterious. Again I edged myself back and decided to stay as far away from both those edges as I could. Then I took a deep breath of fresh air.

"Boy," I said. "Does that ever feel good. You have no idea how stuffy it gets in that pack of yours. Don't you think it's time you threw away some of those old Kleenexes? Not to mention that half-eaten apple down there." I didn't bother to tell her I'd taken a nibble or two of it as a morning snack. Let her feel bad about it.

"Apple? Oh, yeah, it was little Markie. He threw it on the ground yesterday. I tell them not to litter, you know, but they forget. I'll clean it out right now."

"About time, if you ask me—I've never seen so much junk in one place in my life. What's *that* for, anyway?" I was talking about those tweezers, which she'd just taken out and was putting down on the well edge beside the toy car. Somehow, she didn't look like the type who cared a lot about what shape her eyebrows were.

"These? These are really good for getting out splinters. I use them all the time."

While Cheryl sorted through the rest of the stuff in her pack, I took the opportunity to case the joint. It was a garden, all right, filled with flowers of every kind. It was pretty, I guess, but kind of unsettling for some reason. I couldn't put my finger on what it was. Something about the air, maybe something about . . .

The sky.

The sky was green.

Last winter, when I went to Stranger country to get my sister Andrea back, the sky there was green. Disgusting, bilious green. Just like this. So I *was* in the land of the Strangers again. Now I knew for sure what I'd been suspecting all along.

The door between Stranger country and our world was supposed to be closed now. And as far as I knew, neither of us had come through any door to get here. But if Cheryl had come here, if this had happened to me, then obviously the door wasn't closed. Our world was threatened. I was threatened.

I was way past being threatened. I was already in it up to my puny little neck.

And it seemed to have something to do with that master of Cheryl's. The guy who brought her here. He was the key. I asked her to tell me about him.

"He's so kind, Johnny. He looks after all the poor orphaned children with nowhere to go. He just brings them here and loves them and cares for them. And he lets me stay here, too, and he asks nothing in return!"

Nothing? She was providing free day care—and from what she told me, doing most of the cooking and all of the housework. Not to mention the splinter-removing.

"Sounds to me like you have a crush on him," I said.

"That's ridiculous," she snapped, giving me a really dirty look. "Totally ridiculous. Why, if I had a crush on *him*, you wouldn't even be—"

She suddenly turned red, and stopped.

"Even be what?"

As I spoke, I could see her tense up. She started pulling things out of the pack at an exceedingly rapid speed and dropping them on the top of the well wall without even looking at them.

"Hey," I said. "Watch what you're doing. That's my whole wardrobe you nearly dropped into the water." I ran over to the edge where my garbage bag full of clothes had landed, trying not to look down as I grabbed it.

I turned around to give her another piece of my mind. Her face was still bright red. It was quite a display—like the most spectacular sunset you've ever seen. I swear I could almost feel the heat from it.

"I don't know how you got here," she said. "I have no idea—none at all."

I hadn't even gotten around to asking her about that. Cheryl had done something, all right. She just didn't want to admit it. But before I could get it out of her, I heard this loud yipping noise. It was a dog, a vicious-looking and very skinny dog, leaping out of the trees at the edge of the garden and galloping toward us with saliva glistening on its teeth and fire in its eyes.

"Duck, Cheryl!" I shouted, as I kneeled down and put my hands over my head. That beast looked real savage. I expected to be punctured or swallowed any minute.

"Don't be silly, Johnny," Cheryl said. "It's not a duck, it's a dog."

Well, ho-ho-ho. She should do the Letterman show maybe.

And it was no time for joking. From under the cover of my arms over my head, I could hear angry growls and feel hot smelly winds blowing over me.

I cautiously looked up to see the dog's wet nose hovering right in front of my face as it breathed sewer gas on me and rumbled away like an air conditioner. I would have barfed if I hadn't been too frightened to think of it.

"He won't hurt you," Cheryl said reassuringly. "It's just Johnny Nesbit."

A monster dog is about to gulp me down whole and Cheryl tells it not to worry about *me* hurting *it*. What was I going to do, get stuck in its throat on the way down and choke it to death?

But the dog did seem to calm down a little. The growling stopped, although the dog kept glaring at me. I stood there shivering, ready to bolt at any moment, trying to choose between being squashed to death on the lawn if I ran one way or drowning in the well if I ran the other. Either would be better than life inside that animal.

"Wh . . . wh . . . who is he?" I quaked.

"He's my friend," she said, still rubbing the fur at its neck. "He's the dog I told you about, Johnny, remember? The one I met back in the park that day, before I came here? I think he lives out there in the forest somewhere, although I don't know how he manages to squeeze his way through the trees. He comes here every day to visit me, almost like he's making sure I'm okay or something."

Then I heard another loud noise—coming from the doorway of the house this time. The dog must have heard it, too, because its ears suddenly pricked up, and its face looked sort of startled, and then it took off like a shot and disappeared around the corner of the house.

And at the exact same time, this whole batch of screaming kids poured out of the cottage and came barreling down a path toward us, calling out Cheryl's name.

And behind them was a man dressed in black with greasy black hair.

Seven

I didn't really get to see the man. In the wink of an eye, Cheryl had grabbed me and was stuffing me into the fanny pack.

Grabbed me with her actual bare sweaty hand. If it hadn't all happened so fast I would have decked her. Well, maybe not decked her—but at least given her a good solid punch to the thumb that would have smarted for some time.

After she dropped me into the pack and I hit the bottom with a bang, she started hurling everything else on top of me. Combs, Kleenexes—even that damn apple again. It was like being in Kansas with Dorothy during the cyclone. I made my way over to a corner of the pack as quickly as I could, on my knees, and huddled over as everything Cheryl owned came plummeting down on top of me.

But it seems Cheryl hadn't moved quickly enough after all.

"What's that, Cheryl?" I heard a little-kid voice say as I tried to push up the huge aspirin bottle that was crushing me. "A G.I. Joe? I want to play with it."

"No, Ashley, it's not a G.I. Joe. Now, let's—"

"It is, it is, and I want it I want it I want it." I suddenly found myself slamming into the wall of the pack, and then, almost immediately, I was pulled in the opposite direction, right into those damned tweezers again. I guessed that the kid was pulling on the pack, and that Cheryl was pulling back. Furthermore, she hadn't had a chance to zip the zipper, and stuff was flying out. I grabbed on to the seam at the bottom of the pack and held on for dear life.

"Stop that, Ashley," a rich deep voice said. Ashley did, immediately, and the aspirin bottle whammed into me.

"Now be a good child, and go and play. You really must try to control them better, my dear."

"Oh, Ashley's no problem," I heard Cheryl say. "Really he isn't, sir. He's just a little rambunctious."

"It's up to you, of course," the deep voice said. "They're in your charge. I just came to tell you I'm off to my morning work now. I don't want to be disturbed."

"I'll make sure you aren't," Cheryl said. Then I heard footsteps walk off down the path toward the house.

"Phew," I said after a bit. "That was a close one. If that creep had found me here, we'd both be goners."

"Johnny, how can you say that? He's *not* a creep."

I couldn't persuade her he was a creep no matter how hard I tried. And you know, it went on like that, or more or less like that, for a long time—a week, or maybe two. I don't know, I totally lost track. It's easy to lose track when you spend most of your time huddled in the dark with nothing to do but nurse your many wounds and bruises.

Cheryl felt it was only safe to let me out for a few minutes while the kids were all busy eating their meals, or at night after they went to bed. So we developed a routine.

She spent most of her day out in the garden chasing after kids who were hitting each other or running after balls they had lost or leaning over to help them blow their noses. I spent most of my day in the pack, being jostled and bumped and bruised and complaining about it.

She'd let me out only during breakfast and lunch and dinner, when the kids were inside. First I'd pee and poop in the grass. Cheryl made me do it over by the trees, so the kids wouldn't walk in it. I pointed out to her that they were probably walking through bigger piles of bird poop all day long, but she insisted.

Then I'd eat and try to have a sensible conversation with her, without any luck ever.

At some point, usually, that dog would show up, and it would growl at me and let Cheryl pet it, until that greasehead boss of Cheryl's appeared, and then it'd be off lickety-split, as fast as it could go. The dog was obviously scared out of its skull of that guy. I tried to tell Cheryl that the dog probably knew something we didn't, but she wasn't having any of it.

Those conversations with Cheryl were so frustrating. I'd try to get her to think about things, to understand the situation, to figure out something we might do to get me out of this mess. To pound some sense into her. I might as well have been talking to a wall. Hey, considering how big she was, I guess I was sort of talking to a wall.

It was like the whole situation didn't surprise her or bother her at all. Like I said, it was as though she was hypnotized.

Not that she ignored me. Other than actually listening to important stuff that really mattered, she paid me all the attention in the world.

She arranged a whole bunch of crumpled-up Kleenexes inside the pack so I'd have a comfortable place to sleep—unused Kleenexes, thank goodness. And she tried—just once—to tuck the pink blanket in around me at bedtime. She never tried that again, and I'm proud to say she had those teeth marks in her finger for some time.

But she did do my laundry—took it away when I wasn't looking one day at breakfast and washed it and hung it out on the line mixed in with the children's doll clothes that she happened to be washing at the same time. Used this yucky scented fabric softener, too, and all my clothes made me sneeze for the next two days.

And she was constantly reminding me to brush my teeth and eat my vegetables and change my socks and my underwear.

Yeah, even my underwear. The girl had no shame. Once, she even asked me if I was regular. Can you believe it? But hey, at least I knew she wasn't sneaking peaks at me while I was doing my stuff out there in the grass.

And once, at night, she lowered a teacup full of warm water into the pack, and made me take a bath.

Oh, yes, Cheryl was paying attention to me, all right. I began to understand why all those Barbie dolls have that look pasted on their faces all the time. You know, that "I'm smiling on the outside but I'm totally pissed off inside" look.

We had all our meals in the garden by the well, underneath that depressing green sky. Cheryl always gave me part of whatever she was having. I'd pass her my plate, and she'd balance it on her finger and then break off a tiny piece of food with her fork and fill my plate with it and pass it back to me. It was a strange diet, all take-out stuff. We had Egg McMuffins for breakfast, burritos and burgers for lunch, pizzas, Kentucky Fried Chicken and meatball subs for dinner. And Cokes and Snapples for drinks.

Which confused me. I mean, we had to be in Stranger country, so where was all that human food coming from?

"I don't know," Cheryl said to me one day as we ate our lunch—a taco salad. It was a hot day, and I was fanning my face with this huge piece of lettuce as we talked. "It's just there waiting for me when I go into the kitchen at mealtime. Still in the take-out boxes and piping hot."

How could it still be piping hot if it came from another world? The really strange thing was, Cheryl was the only one who got the take-out stuff. The children all ate something else.

I found that out when I finally got to see them eating. Got to see them in general.

It wasn't through any fault of Cheryl's. She was determined to keep me in the fanny pack and keep me a secret. She didn't want her master to find out I was there and get mad at her, and she was afraid the kids would say something to him if they saw me.

It was ridiculous for her to worry about that, because as far as I could tell, he had hardly anything to do with those kids. Or with Cheryl. Oh, sure, he talked to her. I'd be lying there dozing in the pack as Cheryl played with the kids out in the garden, and I'd hear this deep greasy voice all of a sudden. He'd tell her what a wonderful job she was doing and what an excellent mother she'd make some day and crap like that, and then he'd be off again, and Cheryl would spend the next three hours telling me how great he was. It's amazing how much adoration she could squeeze out of one or two greasy sentences from that smooth-talking jerk. He had her just where he wanted her. The poor girl must have been starved for attention. What she really needed was someone to tuck her in and worry about *her* underwear for a while. That would cure her.

I actually asked her one day if *she'd* remembered to change *her* undies. But all she did was giggle and tell me how cute I was. I have to tell you, I was developing more sympathy for Barbie by the minute.

Cheryl didn't know what that master of hers was doing between his quick trips to the garden to ooze some of his grease on her. She thought he spent most of his time working in his office, a room she wasn't allowed to enter, but she wasn't sure.

But even if the guy was never around, there was no way she was going to let me out of that pack to see what was happening. So finally I took matters into my own hands.

It took me a few hours, and a lot of muscle, and I was totally exhausted by the time I finished. But I did it. I made a hole in the canvas wall of the fanny pack with Cheryl's eyebrow tweezers. Just a little hole—one Cheryl and the kids would never notice. But big enough for me to see through.

I did most of the work at night while Cheryl was sleeping, but I didn't actually manage to punch my way through the canvas until after breakfast the next morning. We were out in the garden by then, and Cheryl was too busy keeping the kids from mauling and killing each other to notice what I was doing. I looked out and saw the kids for the first time.

It was no big deal. They looked perfectly normal. Just as normal as they'd sounded before I could see them, just like any group of kids you'd find playing in a school playground.

But then I started noticing things.

Like for instance, they all seemed to live in some sort of fantasy world.

First off, I noticed this one little boy, a skinny red-haired kid with freckles. He was waving his fist in the air and shouting, "I hate you, Nora, I hate you, I hate you. I'm never going to play with you again!" The only thing was, there wasn't anybody there for him to hate and not play with. He was standing all by himself in the middle of the garden.

Jeez, I thought as I watched him do his act. That red-haired kid has some imagination. It was like he was living in a whole different world inside his mind.

But then another kid caught my eye. A girl this time. She was chatting away as she strolled down the path with her arm stuck out into the air beside her. It was as if the arm was draped over the shoulder of a friend that she was telling a long involved story to. Except there was no friend there. There was nobody there but her.

And as I kept on watching, I realized they were all doing it. It was creepy. Especially there in that garden. Because with all that foliage everywhere, and under that revolting green sky, those kids looked sort of green themselves—their skin, I mean.

It wasn't until the next morning at breakfast that I realized it wasn't the sky that was making them look so green.

It was the green beans.

I already knew that Cheryl was the one who prepared the kids' food and put it out on the plates for them. What I didn't know before I made the hole in the pack was what it was she gave them. Green beans. She was feeding them green beans for breakfast.

Green beans, you know, are what Strangers always eat. Last winter, in Stranger country, the queen had tried to trick me into eating their food, but I'd had a warning from a friend, and I didn't eat it, and that's why I was able to escape from there and get back home again. It seems that when human beings eat those Stranger green beans, they get green and turn into Strangers themselves.

Well, these kids sure seemed like human kids to me— or they would have if they hadn't all been giants. But they were in Stranger country, and they were eating green beans, and their skin was looking pretty green already, even inside the house. Something had to be done for sure. Maybe it was too late already.

The last straw was the ointment. See, when I went to Stranger country last year, I went there to get this stuff to put in my parents' eyes. They were under some kind of spell, and without that stuff in their eyes they'd never be able to see that the thing in my sister Andrea's crib wasn't really Andrea at all, just some lazy Stranger who'd taken her place—a changeling, he was called. And guess what I saw Cheryl do right after breakfast? That's right— put ointment in each of the kids' eyes.

I should have guessed it. I'd heard her from inside the pack, lining them up and telling them to be still. But I'd never thought much about what she was doing.

Something bad was happening to these kids—just as bad as what had already happened to me. Not to mention Cheryl. And I couldn't even get Cheryl to see there was a problem. And if she didn't see a problem, nothing was going to happen to solve the problem. How could I get her to see it?

I was so busy thinking about it later that morning that I hardly even noticed it when the next strange thing happened. I was inside the pack, kind of watching this little girl named Sabrina through my peephole as I worried about Cheryl. This Sabrina was playing with an imaginary friend, just like they all were doing. But Sabrina was playing ball, and she was using a real ball—a ball I could actually see.

Sabrina threw the ball. It flew through the air and then, suddenly, it stopped. Just came to a complete halt in midair. Just as if somebody had actually caught it.

I nearly jumped out of my skin when I saw that—and Cheryl, of course, was looking right at it and didn't even notice. But what happened next was worse. The ball twisted around in the air, and then, suddenly, it came flying right back to Sabrina.

Somehow, Sabrina had managed to have her imaginary friend actually catch the ball and throw it back to her.

Maybe, I told myself after I got over the shock, the friend wasn't so imaginary after all. Maybe the friend was there, and it was me who couldn't see her. Or him. Or it.

Well, there was only one way to find out.

Cheryl kept the tube of ointment in her pack, of course, along with just about everything else she owned. Along with me. It was a simple matter of climbing over to the tube and opening it up and putting some of the goop on my eyes and then taking another look through my peephole.

Or it would have been a simple matter if the cap on that tube hadn't been the size of my head and screwed on so tight that it was impossible to turn. Finally, I had to use my trusty tweezers again to punch a hole in the side of the tube. Just a little hole, but big enough so that when I took a jump onto the tube, I managed to squeeze out more than enough ointment for my eyes.

And saw just what I expected to see. Invisible kids, but they were visible to me now. Visible and very, very green. The kids I'd been able to see before weren't acting at all. They'd been playing with real friends, not imaginary ones. Friends I hadn't been able to see without the ointment. Stranger friends.

Stranger friends Cheryl couldn't see and didn't even know were there. Every once in a while, one of the invisible kids would come over and hug Cheryl, or give her a kiss, and then go off and play again. Of course, the ordinary kids were doing that, too, all the time. But it seemed different when the kids who were clambering all over her were the green ones. She was being kissed and hugged over and over again by invisible people without even knowing it. Talk about creepy.

And who were those green kids, anyway? How could a bunch of very green Strangers be so fond of Cheryl? How did they know her when she couldn't even see them? Another conundrum.

But this one I solved fairly easily, at lunchtime, as

Cheryl and I took up our usual positions at the well. The garden was just as empty as it always was at mealtime—the green kids must have been back in the kitchen with the others, scarfing down their beans. I guess just because you're green and invisible doesn't mean you don't have to eat.

"So tell me," I asked Cheryl in between nibbles of the fry I was holding with both hands. "These kids you look after. Have any of them disappeared or anything?"

Cheryl gulped down a fry and then gave me a funny look. "It's strange you should mention that," she said. "I hadn't really thought about it, but yes, they have—well, not disappeared, exactly. That sounds so evil. But some of them have gone away. Lots of them. Just this morning, I noticed that little Markie wasn't here. Just gone. Now, why have I never thought about that?" She paused for a moment, a perplexed look on her face.

Why indeed? And I bet she'd even forget we'd ever had this conversation about two minutes after we finished having it.

"In fact," she went on, "they keep going away all the time. Hardly a day goes by without one of them just vanishing. I mean, there was Ryan and little Suze and Jerry and Jane and Marcia and . . . and tons of others. What's happened to them all?" She grabbed another fry and chewed on it thoughtfully.

"Maybe," she continued, "I didn't notice it all that much because there are always the same *number* of kids? I mean, like today, Markie's gone, but now little Claire is here instead. She was there this morning when I woke up, instead of Markie. Whenever a kid goes away, there's always another kid to take their place. So there's always fifteen kids—one for each bed. Anyway, Johnny, it's the master's business, not ours. He asked me to look after the kids, not to start acting like some private eye asking dumb questions. And he's a nice man. Wherever he's taking the kids when they leave here, it can't be anywhere bad. Let's talk about something else."

She had to be hypnotized.

After lunch, I nestled down into my Kleenexes in the dark and tried to sort it all out. It had to go something like this. That greaseball master of Cheryl's was a Stranger, and he was stealing kids—human kids. He was feeding them green beans to turn them into Strangers and putting ointment in their eyes so they could see other Strangers.

Why? That I didn't know.

But Cheryl wasn't getting any green beans. He got Big Macs and stuff for her, so he obviously had other plans for her. Most likely the plans consisted just of keeping her human so she could go on being a nanny and a housekeeper and general all-round slave as he trundled kids through this Stranger-making assembly line of his.

Which was a good thing, in one way at least. Because maybe it was too late for some of those kids. They were Strangers already. But if Cheryl hadn't eaten any of the Stranger food, it meant there was still a chance for her. And me, too—because I was eating what she was eating.

Cheryl obviously hadn't been getting any of the ointment, either, probably so the changed kids would be invisible to her and she wouldn't start asking any questions.

Not that she was all that likely to ask questions. He'd made sure of that, too, somehow. She wasn't going to start asking questions until she saw what was really going on. Saw it literally, with her own two giant eyes.

My next step was clear.

Eight

That very night, as soon as the buzz-saw sounds coming from the other side of the wall of the pack told me that Cheryl was sound asleep, I got to work. I wedged the end of Cheryl's comb between the aspirin bottle and a box of cough drops, leaned it against the wall of the pack, climbed up, and started to unzip the zipper.

I had to go down and move the comb about four times before I finally managed to get the zipper open enough for me to crawl through the opening. After I made it past the sharp edges of the zipper pieces, it was a simple matter of tying my shoelace through the hole in the zipper handle, lowering myself down onto the bed, and then tiptoeing across the pillow.

Then came the hard part. I had to crawl up over Cheryl's shoulder and along her neck and her cheeks to her eyes. That's right—I had to get on her face. It had to be done, so

I did it. I got out the extra pair of socks I was carrying in my pants pocket, put them on my hands, and I did it.

Lucky she was a strong sleeper. You'd think I would at least have tickled a little, but she was so busy snoring she didn't even move.

It took all my willpower to make myself crawl on her like that. I mean, sure, getting close to people can be nice, but this was ridiculous.

And if that wasn't bad enough, there was the snoring. At that range, it sounded like a hurricane in full force, and it would have felt like one, too, if I'd allowed myself anywhere near the gale that was emerging from her open mouth—a gale with more than a hint of garlic in it that was noticeable even way over by the ear. I just gritted my teeth and kept right on crawling.

The hardest part was getting at her eyes. They were closed so tightly that it took all my strength to force the lids apart.

But after that, it was easy. I'd gooped up my hand with a whole bunch of the ointment before I left home. So I just took off the sock, opened my fist, jabbed my hand in, and rubbed away. It was sort of like cleaning windows.

At which point she woke up. Well, I guess you'd wake up too if somebody poked you in the eye and started housecleaning.

Fortunately, she didn't wake up all the way, and she immediately fell asleep again. Or so I guessed. I couldn't see for sure from where I'd fallen, down below on the pillow. Lucky for me it was a soft mattress.

Anyway, I didn't hang around to find out. Holding the shoelace, I shinnied myself up the side of the pack, zipped myself back in, and then quickly climbed under the pink blanket on my own bed. I'd have to wait until morning to see if it worked.

It worked. It worked real good.

Nothing happened until we were in the kitchen. There weren't any green kids in the bedroom, and I figured they must have been sleeping somewhere else. Well, they had green thumbs, didn't they? Maybe they had a garden bed. Ho ho.

Anyway, I could hear Cheryl slopping beans out onto the kids' plates and telling them to keep their elbows off the table. All of a sudden she shrieked, and I could hear the crash as the bowl of beans hit the floor.

She'd seen a whole bunch of green kids come pouring into the room. Now, along with the only mildly greenish kids she expected to be there, there were two or three very green ones perched on each chair. The joint was crawling with pigmentally challenged children.

Furthermore, she knew them all. After she got past staring at their skin and started to make out some details, she began calling out their names. Which pleased them all no end, because it was the first time Cheryl had paid any attention to them since they'd become invisible to her. They all came running over to hug her, and she hugged them back, which made them all want to hug her even more, and I got jostled even worse than usual.

"Cheryl," I shouted at the top of my voice as I tumbled around inside the pack, "watch out. Jeez. What's happening out there?" Nobody heard me, of course. By this time, the green kids were asking Cheryl why she'd been ignoring them for so long, and she was telling them she hadn't been ignoring them because they hadn't even been there, and they were saying oh yes they had been there and stop teasing, Cheryl—and they went on like that, for hours. I had to wait until lunchtime in the garden to actually talk to her about it.

Or rather, listen to her. She started in even before she had finished unzipping the pack.

"Johnny," she said, "you'll never guess what happened! The children who went away? They've come back!"

"Wrong, Cheryl," I said as I tied the good old shoelace around my middle. "They've been here all along. See, it's—"

But she wasn't listening. "Or rather, they've been here all along, they say, except for some reason I couldn't see them! Strange, eh? But they're all here! Ryan and little Suze and Jerry and Jane and Marcia and all the others, too!"

She kept right on talking as she fished me out of the pack and carelessly dropped me down onto the well edge with a large thump. "I told you he wouldn't hurt them or anything, didn't I? They're all perfectly fine." Then she paused for a brief moment. "Well, there is just this one little thing. Their skin, it's sort of . . . well, it's green."

I nodded.

"You're not surprised?"

"Nope," I said. "A lot of them have green skin."

"Them?"

"Yeah, them. Strangers."

She looked totally bewildered. I decided I'd better break it to her gently.

"Like this one I knew," I explained. "A guy named Liam. He was in our class last year. It was before you came, so you never met him. Well, *he* was one of them, a Stranger. But he'd wandered out of Stranger country into our world. And his skin was green, too, just like these kids. But then he, well, disappeared. And that's why—"

"Honestly, Johnny, I don't know what you're talking about. Strangers? More people disappearing? Are you feeling okay? Let me feel your forehead."

"Look, Cheryl," I said, stepping back from her outstretched thumb, "now that you see those kids, surely you understand that . . ."

But she wasn't paying any attention to me. Her face had gone dead white, and she was staring down past me, into the well.

I rushed over as close to the edge as I dared to go on my feet, then got down on my hands and knees and inched myself right to the very edge and looked over.

At first, all I could see was the sunlight glinting on the top of the water, making it look like the world's largest cubic zirconia. Then my eyes adjusted.

There were creatures in there, under the water.

Not fish or water bugs or anything like that. People.

Tiny perfectly formed people no bigger than water bugs.

Or at least, some of them were people. Some of the others, I began to realize, were something else. Some of them had two heads. Some just seemed to be like flames in the shape of human bodies, floating around skeletons, and some were just empty dresses that seemed to be dancing with empty suits of armor.

Strangers, of course—just like the ones I'd seen in the queen's castle last winter. And they were dancing the way they did in that castle.

Furthermore, one of the creatures who was dancing looked especially familiar. It was a woman wearing a dress covered with jewels and with this diamond tiara thing on her head, like the queen of England wears. If she hadn't been so small and inside a well, she'd have been a dead ringer for the Stranger queen.

So small? She wasn't any smaller than I myself was. Maybe she *was* the Stranger queen. And if that nasty queen was part of all this mess . . .

She sure did seem to be. I could see her down there, dancing with a creature that looked like a man, a tiny ordinary human man with very shiny dark hair and a carefully trimmed little beard. He looked sort of familiar, too, but I couldn't place him. Nobody I knew ever put that much grease in their hair.

As I stared down through the water trying to figure out how I knew him, he looked straight into the face of the woman in the tiara and gave her this dazzling smile.

"It is!" Cheryl suddenly said. "I thought it was. I recognized that smile right away. It's him. The master."

"That's the guy you're working for here? That greasehead?"

"It's him, all right. But it can't be. He's way too small. He's as small as you. How—?" She stared down in utter bewilderment.

It was bewildering. If that little guy down there was actually Cheryl's life-size boss, then the rest must be life-size, too. Including the queen. It was some trick of magic or something that just made them look small. To them, the surface of the water on top of the well must look like a huge ceiling. A pretty glittery ceiling, when the sunlight shone on it.

Last year, the ceiling in the Stranger castle had glittered just like that.

As I tried to figure it all out, I found myself wondering what would happen if I just jumped into the well. I mean, assuming that what we could see down there wasn't just some kind of illusion or magic trick, assuming I didn't just drown—when I made it down to the bottom, would I be my normal size? Or would I just be a little doll to them, too, like I was to Cheryl?

Well, I wasn't about to find out. I could just imagine what that queen would do if I suddenly came hurtling down into her party like that. She wasn't the kind of person who'd be tolerant of party crashers.

Cheryl was still staring into the well. "What's he doing in there, anyway? How did he—?"

She turned to me, an urgent look on her face.

"Johnny, I don't get it. What's happening? The kids showing up again, the master the size of a water bug and down in the well, those—those things all dancing, you here, and you're so puny, too. And the sky is green. I don't get it. Why is everything so strange?"

It was like a fog suddenly disappearing all at once. Cheryl wasn't hypnotized anymore. She was suddenly seeing things clearly.

Very clearly. "And all that goop in his hair. Yuck. How could I have ever thought he was nice? I bet the only reason he even let me come here in the first place was because he needed a servant. Oh, Johnny, I have been so dumb."

What could I say? It was true. I just looked at her and nodded. Embarrassed, Cheryl turned away from me, back toward those creatures in the well.

The dancing had stopped, and that master of Cheryl's had his head bent over the queen's hand, kissing it (and probably dripping a pound or two of grease on it as a bonus). Then he led her over to a fancy chair on a raised platform.

As soon as the queen sat down, the master guy looked up, right at us. And then he started to grow. He got bigger and bigger, as if he was zooming up to the surface of the water. Soon his body almost filled the well, and he got still closer—like someone just about to be shot out of a cannon. I expected him to just suddenly pop up through the surface of the water and grab both of us and break our necks for spying on him.

But he didn't. Instead, just as he got to be almost life-size and looked like he was barely under the surface of the water and I was ducking my head under my arm and beginning to pray, he disappeared. Like a TV being turned off.

Then, not three seconds later, the door of the house opened, and the exact same guy stepped out into the garden, the sun glinting off his greasy head, and smiled that toothy smile, and said, "Lovely morning, isn't it, Cheryl, my dear?" And then he stepped back in the house. He hadn't even looked at Cheryl closely enough to notice the startled expression on her face, or to see little old me standing there beside her. What a phony.

But at least Cheryl knew he was a phony now. The ointment had done its work. Now we could begin to make some plans.

Nine

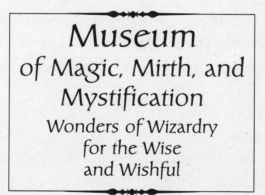

Museum
of Magic, Mirth, and Mystification
Wonders of Wizardry
for the Wise
and Wishful

The sign was over the top of an archway. And behind it, in an alcove, was a wall covered with shelves. Shelves full of things, crowded together and coated with dust but carefully arranged, and all with little signs to go with them, all in the same strange letters. It looked exactly like what the sign said—a museum. A dusty museum nobody had visited for a couple of centuries.

"See," Cheryl said, "I told you they were here." She lowered the candle and walked under the archway.

We were back in the room where she'd first found me inside the bottle. If I leaned over far to the right and craned my neck I could even see the bottle, glinting there in the darkness in the middle of all its bottle buddies.

I could see it because Cheryl was letting me stick my head out of the pack. She figured it was safe, because the kids were all asleep, and it was pitch-dark out. At first, I'd been standing on the comb to get high enough to see out. But as soon as Cheryl started walking in that galumphing giant lope of hers, the comb slid away from under my feet, and now I was dangling there in midair with the sharp edges of the zipper teeth sticking into my armpits. It was worth the pain. I could actually see for once.

It had taken Cheryl all afternoon to remember this museum place. We spent hours trying to think of something to do—Cheryl sitting on the well edge watching the green kids play with the not-so-green kids, me sitting inside in the dark and occasionally shouting ideas up at her. But we kept coming up blank.

We couldn't figure where to start. There were too many different things to worry about. There were those green kids, not to mention the ones who weren't quite so green yet. Could any of them be de-greened somehow? After all, my old buddy Liam had gradually become less green in the time I'd known him. But these were humans turning into Strangers, not vice versa. Was there still a chance to save them? And how could we save them if we didn't know exactly what it was we were trying to save them from? Like, who *was* that greaseball master of Cheryl's, and what exactly was he doing here? And *why* was he doing it?

And then, as I kept having to remind Cheryl, there was me. I really did kind of want to become my normal size again.

There was also the small matter of figuring out where we were and how we got here and getting us all back home—assuming, of course, there still was a home to get back to. Maybe that greaseball had just stuffed the whole universe down his garden well.

"It's not fair," Cheryl said. "*He* knows everything, and we don't know anything. He holds all the cards. How are we ever going to get out of this mess?"

Good question. I was so lost in thought, I hadn't even realized I'd gotten to my feet and wandered over the humps of Kleenex to the little hole I'd made in the side of the pack. I took a peek out. I was facing the well, and if I closed my eyes real tight, I could just barely make out the sparkles of the sun, still glinting on the well water. Not a dancing creature in sight, though. The Stranger castle was gone from view.

"Too bad we weren't actually *in* the Stranger castle," I called out to Cheryl. "The queen there, she owes me one. And she has all this magic stuff—things that could help us to get the kids out, probably."

She shrieked so loud I jumped. "Magic stuff! But Johnny, there *is* stuff like that! Right here!"

That's when she told me about the museum, and we decided to visit it as soon as we could—that very night, as soon as the kids were all asleep.

And now here we were. We'd been a little worried it might be just a closet again, but it wasn't. We didn't know what we expected to find, exactly. But there had to be something that could help us somehow.

Flinching a little as some of my armpit hairs got razored by the zipper teeth of the fanny pack, I looked over at the shelves. There were cups, stones, pieces of clothing. Nothing special to look at, but if half of what those little signs said was true, then appearances were deceiving. The cups would make you smart, the torn old shirts would make you strong.

"Jeez," I said. "It's like a garage sale at a witch's house. There's got to be something in all this mess that can— Ouch! Watch what you're doing."

Cheryl had leaned over all of a sudden to take a closer look at something on a low shelf, and I'd nearly flipped out of the bag—right down onto the floor about a mile below. I'd have made one magnificent splat falling from that height.

"Look," I said, after my heart started beating again, "why don't you just put me down somewhere before you do me in altogether? Anyway, trying to read those signs while I'm bobbing up and down like this is going to make me carsick for sure. Or, I guess, packsick."

She put me down on one of the shelves, in front of a mangy-looking animal skin of some sort that looked like a high cliff to me. The sign beside it said it was a sealskin. No wonder people objected to killing seals if that's what the coats ended up looking like and smelling like. The sign also said the skin once belonged to a sea creature who took it off and turned into a human being.

Goody for it. How was that supposed to help us?

"Oh, look, Johnny," Cheryl said from further down the shelf. "Isn't this sweet?"

I walked down to see what she was looking at. A glass shoe that supposedly once belonged to a dancing elf.

"It's just like the shoe in 'Cinderella,'" she said. "And look"—she pointed at my foot, giggling a little—"it's exactly your size."

Big deal. What did she expect me to do, put the shoe on and scare her master to death with a clear view of my knobby toes? "And how's *that* supposed to help us?"

"It's not, but—" She giggled even more.

"What's so funny?"

"Nothing," she said, trying to stop the giggles. "It's just that, well—I suddenly had this picture of you wearing that shoe and, like, dressed up in a fancy princess gown like Cinderella on the way to the ball. A"—and she giggled yet again—"a dress with pink ruffles."

Ho ho ho. So funny I forgot to laugh. I decided to just ignore her and continue my stroll.

The next thing I passed was a perfectly ordinary-looking heap of stones—sort of like gravel, but the pieces were each about the size of my head. The sign by them said:

These sharpish stones, so gray and flimsy,
Once used to be the giant Grimsey;
Off a cliff poor Grim did travel
And ended up a pile of gravel.
Rub the stones, if that's your whim—
They'll turn once more back into Grim.

"Just what we need," I said. "More giants."

There didn't seem to be anything helpful on that shelf. I asked Cheryl to move me up to the next one.

"I looked at that stuff already," she said, "the first time I was here. Before I found you in the bottle. *Exactly* before—" She stopped in midsentence, a strange look on her face. "Anyway," she went on, "there's nothing useful on it. Nothing at all." And she picked me up by the waist with her fingers without even asking me and dumped me down on the next shelf up past that one.

What was going on in that strange head of hers now? Well, there was no time to worry about it, because this shelf seemed more promising.

"This might be good," Cheryl said, pointing at the leather purse she'd plopped me down in front of. The sign beside it said:

To fill your mouth and stuff your gullet
Open up this wondrous wallet;
Open up and let it spill—
After empty it will fill.

"Just imagine," Cheryl said, "you'd always have enough

to feed your children, no matter how close it was to welfare check day. Their little tummies would always be full."

Welfare check day? Boy, I thought, Cheryl must have some kind of home life back in Winnipeg. No wonder she was so willing to be tricked by that greaseball. And I'd been thinking she was just plain dumb.

Well, hey, maybe she *was* dumb. She was picking up the purse.

"No," I shouted. "Don't pick it up. Not until we've thought it through. It could be dangerous."

But she didn't put it down. "I don't see how a little purse could be dangerous. And if it actually worked—" By now she was actually opening the purse and peering inside. "There is!" she shouted gleefully. "There's a cheese sandwich inside! Cheddar with lettuce on white— my favorite. See?"

She took something out of the purse and waved it in my face. Cheddar, all right.

"And hey!" she said, dropping the sandwich in her excitement. "There's another one inside!"

By the time I'd levered the first sandwich off my head, Cheryl was going wild, madly pulling cheese sandwiches out of the purse and shrieking, "Another! And another! And another!"

No matter how many she took out, there was always another one inside. As far as I could tell, in the brief instant I got to see each one before she tossed it over her shoulder and reached in for the next, they were all cheddar on white with lettuce.

A Completely Different Place   93

"It works," she screeched, turning toward me as she still wildly pulled cheese sandwiches out of the purse.

I gave her a cold look. "So what are you going to do, bury that boss of yours in cheese sandwiches?"

"Boss?" She suddenly stopped shrieking and pulled her hand out of the bag. "Oh, yeah. The master." She dropped the sandwich she was holding and looked at me, confused.

"For a moment there," she finally said, "I forgot why we were here. The children. *Him*. All I could think of was sandwiches."

"I told you, Cheryl," I said, kneeling down and looking over the edge at the huge pile of cheese sandwiches strewn on the floor around her feet. "This stuff is dangerous. We have to think before we act."

"I will, from now on. I promise." She put the purse back on the shelf.

"Good," I said, and I went over and began to tug on the first cheese sandwich, the one that Cheryl had conked me with. It was blocking my path, and I figured it might as well join its buddies down below.

As I tugged on it, I began to notice how good it smelled. I don't usually like white bread, or cheese, but it had been hours since the chicken fajitas we'd had for supper. Without even thinking about it, I reached down, grabbed a fistful of sandwich, and put it in my mouth.

It tasted great.

But for a tiny bite, it sure did seem to be filling up a lot of my mouth. In fact, it seemed to be growing.

Growing a lot. It was like this wad of cheese sandwich was gradually expanding, growing down my throat, suffocating me, choking me.

"Take it out!" I heard Cheryl's voice shrieking as I tried to breathe. "Right now!"

Take it out? Open my mouth and reach in and grab the piece of food I was chewing and take it out? In front of her?

But, I told myself as I choked, it really wasn't any time to worry about manners. Gasping for breath, I reached into my mouth and grabbed hold of the half-chewed food and dragged it out. And stood there gagging a little.

"We have to think before we act," Cheryl said as my breath returned to normal. "To quote an expert." She was peering down at me with this snide smile on her face, looking very superior.

But she was right. I mean *I* was right. This stuff worked. That sandwich did exactly what the sign said. It filled my mouth and stuffed my gullet. You had to think really carefully about what the words on the signs meant.

I resolved to be more careful, cleared my throat one more time, and started to look for something more practical, and less tricky.

But Cheryl had already found something. "Now this," she said, "is exactly what he deserves."

I walked *around* the rest of the sandwich, making sure not to touch it, and ambled down toward where she stood. And stopped dead in my tracks.

She was looking at a sword that was leaning against the back wall of the shelf.

It was one scary-looking monster, that sword. It had a long blade, about twice as long as her arm—and I could see it was very sharp. If I happened to trip and fall on that thing, I'd be lying there in two equal halves. Beside its jewel-encrusted hilt, there was a sign—just a little one:

Take up the sword—foes quail, then flee:
A mighty savage you will be!

And, you know, that's just the way Cheryl looked as she stared at the sign—savage.

"This would make me really dangerous," she said, and she was reaching out for the sword even as she said it, as if she'd totally forgotten all about that sandwich. It had to be part of the magic.

"Cheryl, don't!" I called out. "Don't do it, please!"

It was too late. She'd already picked up the sword.

"Put it down!"

"I can't," she shrieked, waving the sword wildly. "It's like it's glued or something. I can't put it down!"

Then her voice changed, grew strangely happy. "And I don't care!" she crowed. "It feels good! And I'm angry—so, so angry! Vengeance, vengeance! Kill! Kill! Kill!"

Jeez. I skedaddled out of there as fast as I could and dived down behind the cheese sandwich. By the time I got up enough courage to peek out again, Cheryl was stomping around, slashing that sword at everything in sight.

"Death," she was crying. "Give me a throat to slit! I want a belly to slash! Kill! Kill kill kill!" She suddenly jabbed at the shelf, and the sword went right through the leather purse she'd dropped there, sending a few hundred more cheese sandwiches raining to the ground. I lifted up the top piece of bread and crawled right in, under the lettuce. Any port in a storm.

"Take that!" Cheryl screeched at some imaginary enemy. "May your blood spill all over! May your heart fall out! May you trip on your own intestines! May there be holes in the holes of your nose!" As I peeked up at her from under the lettuce, I could tell from the look on her face that she was enjoying herself immensely.

But imaginary enemies weren't good enough, apparently. Now she was sniffing the air.

"Blood," she said in a low evil voice. "I smell human blood. Johnny Nesbit, you little rat! Where are you, you creep? I know you're here somewhere. Come out and taste your medicine, you vermin, you toad, you rat, you piece of phlegm!"

Calling me ever nastier names and sniffing the air, she moved toward me, sword ready to thrust, closer, closer, closer—

And suddenly she went sliding downward. First her head, then the arm waving the sword dropped past the edge of the shelf and out of sight.

Dead silence. After a moment or two, I couldn't stand it anymore. I had to see. I crawled out from under the lettuce and went to the edge and looked down.

Thank goodness for those cheese sandwiches. As Cheryl moved toward me, screaming about killing, she must have slipped on one and went sliding forward out of my view. And as she did it, the sword fell out of her hand.

Now she was lying in a pile of squished cheese and bread, looking very silly. And very embarrassed.

"Cheryl," I said, glaring right into her sheepish eyes. "I have seen scary things in my life. I have had encounters with evil Strangers. I have spent an entire lunch hour in the cafeteria of Churchill High and lived to tell the tale. Hell, I once even had my mother sneak up on me while I was washing whites and coloreds in the same load. But that business with the sword was the very scariest thing I have ever seen in my entire life. You have to promise me that you will never, ever pick up one of these magic things without carefully thinking about it first. Promise—right now."

"Okay, okay," she mumbled, her eyes downcast. "I promise." For a large person, she was looking very small. And for a small person, I was feeling pretty large for a change. And enjoying it.

"Good," I added. "Let's just hope all that shouting didn't wake up that greasy boss of yours. He could come bursting in any minute and put you in front of a firing squad. Or make you eat a cheese sandwich."

I could tell from the look on her face that whatever choice he made she knew she deserved it. But as it happened, the guy must have been a sound sleeper. He never did come.

"We're obviously going about this the wrong way," I said. "I mean, it's going to take some real thinking, some real *careful* thinking. We need a plan."

So we started at one end of the top shelf. I was going to walk down the shelf, Cheryl following me but standing on the ground with the little notebook and ridiculously sharp pencil she kept in the fanny pack, making notes for future reference. As we came to each item, we'd each read the sign. Not out loud, of course—we knew how dangerous that might be. Then we'd think carefully—as carefully as we could—about what it meant. And Cheryl would make notes.

"An envelope," I called out. It was just an ordinary white envelope, one that would have been the size of an ordinary letter to Cheryl. But the sign said there was a whole lake in it. I could tell there was, too, because when I put my ear up close to it (being careful not to actually touch it, of course), I could hear the waves. It sounded like Grand Beach on a windy day in there.

"Hmm," I said. "We could drown him with it, maybe."

"Yeah," she answered, "and drown ourselves, too. Unless," she added, catching sight of the next thing on the shelf, "we used this."

Cheryl was looking at a ratty-looking sheepskin vest with a sign that said you'd never get tired swimming while you wore it.

"That might work," I said. "You could put it on and tuck me inside it. And then you could call him in here and get the letter out and make the lake and we'd be swimming and—"

"No good. What about the kids?"

The kids. I'd forgotten about them, but now I could see them in my mind, spread out over the surface of a vast lake like bright green seaweed twisting in the water as they drowned.

Next was a bottle containing servants that came out and set a table with gold dishes. Great if you were having the prime minister over for dinner, we decided, but not much use in dealing with a sweet-talking bad guy.

Then another bottle containing servants, but these ones came out and beat up on everyone in sight. Better— but everybody in sight would include *us*, of course. That one we didn't even have to think twice about.

After that there was a whole shelf full of stuff like pitchers that poured out money and stones that turned everything to gold and rings that made you rich beyond your wildest dreams. Totally useless.

Next was an ointment that cured all diseases. "Also totally useless," I said. But Cheryl remembered that green skin the kids had, and she made a note about the ointment for future reference.

Then there was a cup filled with some murky-looking liquid. The sign said:

> In this cup, all tightly curled,
> Is all the knowledge of the world.
> Take a drop and know a bit;
> Drink it all and have ALL wit.

"If I drank that," Cheryl said in a sad voice, "maybe I wouldn't do such dumb things all the time, like with that sword, and . . . and . . ." She paused for a moment, thinking, I suppose, about something she didn't want to tell me. "Well," she finally said, "maybe I wouldn't make so much trouble for everybody all the time."

How could she imagine she was stupid? I could tell from the careful way she was thinking about all this stuff that she wasn't stupid. But the expression on her face as she looked at that cup was hungry, very hungry.

"Don't do it, Cheryl," I said. "Please don't."

"But how could having knowledge ever be a bad thing?"

"Think about it," I urged. "I mean, hunger, war, murder. Strangers. Language Arts. There are too many awful things to know about."

"I . . . I suppose so. But . . ."

"Let's get moving," I said, heading off down the shelf to distract her from that cup. "What's next?"

It was a stone of invisibility. If you held it, nobody could see you. We decided it might be useful, even though we couldn't figure out how. We also decided not to forget about a harp that made people feel calm when they heard its music, and a fiddle that made you dance when it was played.

The harp might come in handy, Cheryl said, if her master found her in there and got mad at her. As for the fiddle, well, I once read this fairy tale about a guy who had a fiddle like that, and he tricked his enemy into the middle of a thornbush and then started to play it. Imagine the agony.

Next was another stone that you could put in your mouth so you could speak and understand all languages. Great—I could just see myself spouting Tagalog or Ojibwa at Cheryl's boss as he performed a spell that turned me into a frog. I could croak in Tagalog.

Yet another stone. This time the little sign said:

> From lies your mouth be shut!
> Just hold me and you'll see:
> What you say shall be
> The truth—and nothing but.

"Terrific," Cheryl said, after I'd read that out to her. "Here we are, trying to fake out a magician—a very powerful magician—and this would stop us from even being able to lie to him. It's going to be hard enough already."

"I don't know," I mused. "'What you say shall be the truth.' Maybe we're missing something there."

"Maybe," she said, not really listening. "But hey, look at this. This one's a definite keeper."

It was armor that protected you against all wounds.

"Yup," I agreed. "That would come in handy, all right, especially if someone got hold of that sword you picked up. Would it fit you?"

We looked more closely. She'd be like a sardine in a tuna can inside of that huge thing. It might have fit me better. If I'd been my normal size, which I wasn't, of course. In my current size I'd be like a sardine in a whale can.

And there didn't seem to be anything to help get me

back to my normal size, either. Some museum of magic this was. Sure, you could speak Lithuanian while eating off gold plates and swimming forever, but when it came to making tiny people the right size, well, you'd just have to do your shopping somewhere else.

We looked over all that stuff and thought about it for what seemed like hours—and we just couldn't seem to come up with any ideas about how to use it. We'd looked at and thought about every single thing on every one of the shelves.

Except the shelf Cheryl hadn't wanted me to look at before.

I had to look at it.

"Maybe you missed something," I said. "I might figure out something you didn't catch."

"That's what I'm afraid of," she mumbled.

I kept on insisting, and finally she agreed. "Have it your own way, then," she said, and plonked me down on the shelf so hard the bottom of my feet hurt.

I could see right away it was just more useless treasure-making stuff. Why was she acting so strangely about it?

Then I saw it.

Ten

It was a big gold round thing with jewels on it—an orb, I guess you call it. The sign beside it said:

To bring your true love to your side,
Just think love's name and be love's guide.
Hold the orb, and love's name think,
Love will answer in a wink.
Love will answer to your call,
Be love big or be it small.

With Cheryl hovering over me looking like she was ready for a nuclear explosion to happen at any instant, it didn't take me long to figure it out.

She'd been here, she said, before I showed up. She'd been looking at the stuff on this very shelf. She'd been mooning over this stuff, and then, all of a sudden, she'd heard me, there inside the bottle.

It could only mean one thing.

She'd brought me here. I knew she had something to do with it, and I was right.

I could almost see her doing it. She'd picked up the orb and thought about—

Oh, jeez. She thought about the name of the guy she loved.

She thought about *my* name.

I felt myself turn just as red as she already was. No wonder she didn't want me to look at that shelf.

"I didn't mean it to happen, Johnny."

I just looked at her. I couldn't think of a thing to say.

"I . . . well," she added, "I thought that all this crazy stuff the signs said couldn't ever really happen. I mean, it's like out of a fairy tale or something. Who would ever have thought it could be real?"

She had a point there.

But it had been real. She really did love . . . jeez.

"Of course, that was before I found out about the green kids. Before I found you. *Exactly* before I . . . but I was just daydreaming. I nearly died when I saw you there in that house. I mean, I don't really l . . . lo . . . I mean, I *like* you and all, sure, I'll admit it. I like you a little, I always have, ever since the first day I came to Churchill and saw your cute smile and . . . Oh, this is *so* embarrassing!"

So she liked me. And I suddenly realized something even more unsettling. I wouldn't have minded, it wouldn't have been so bad, if I didn't sort of like her, too.

In the time we'd been together there, I'd grown to like her a lot.

How embarrassing.

But she liked me just a *little*, she said. So it was that tricky Stranger magic, taking advantage of poor Cheryl and her dumb daydreams. Twisting everything around, making people suffer. Making them get into horrible conversations just like the one Cheryl and I were having at this very moment.

Hey, wait a minute. Tricky magic. "A little," she'd said. Was that why I was so small? "Be love big or be it small," the poem said. Did that mean the person would come in the size of the love you felt?

What if you loved someone so much they came as large as an elephant and squashed you?

But Cheryl loved me just a little, so I was little. It was both a good thing and a bad thing. The bad thing was being little. The good thing was that she didn't really have the hots for me all that much. I mean, sure, I liked her and all. I wasn't exactly ready for any kind of major commitment—like, for instance, mentioning a single word about how I felt about her to anybody at all, ever. Especially Cheryl.

There was only one thing to do. I tried to forget how embarrassed I was, and I told Cheryl it really wasn't her fault and let's just forget about it and go back to thinking about the museum stuff.

And we did. Now that I knew what had brought me here, I knew for sure that there had to be a way to get me back. We just had to figure out what it was.

But we couldn't.

"I'm stumped," Cheryl finally announced an hour or so later.

"Me, too," I said, pacing back and forth along a shelf at Cheryl's eye level. "But there's got to be a way, I know there is. If only we could get our heads straight, think more clearly—there's a way to do it, if only we knew what it was."

Cheryl nodded. "If only we knew," she repeated, and then her face suddenly lit up. "Johnny, that's it!"

"Huh?"

"That's it—knowing more! That cup, remember? 'Take a drop and know a bit,' it said. So how much you know depends on how much you drink. And we don't want to know very much, not compared to all the things there are to know—just how to get out of this mess. And, well, *you* obviously couldn't drink any of it, you being so very small. I mean, one drop would be like a whole big glassful to you. Through no fault of your own, of course." She stopped a moment and gave me a panicky look, which I did my very best to ignore.

"But me," she hastily continued, "I could do it. I wouldn't have to drink much, only a little drop or two. And then, well, maybe I'd know enough to figure something out. Some way to do it."

"Yeah, sure," I said. "Some way to kill us all. It's too risky."

But eventually, you know, I had to let her do it,

because no matter how long I sat there and squeezed my brain, I couldn't think of anything else.

"It's your funeral," I finally said. "And just remember it was *your* idea, not mine."

She took just the teeniest of sips to begin with, as I watched her anxiously. "Well," I said impatiently, "what's happening? Do you feel different? Do you know more?"

"An intriguing and thought-provoking inquiry," she said. "Ultimately, of course, such esoteric but decidedly nonauxiliary inquiries into the metaphysical (not to mention metalogical) ramifications of the human (and for that matter animal) existence adumbrate many philosophical, moral, and ethical uncertainties, particularly in the post-Derridean *Weltanschauung*, all of which indubitably center around the issue of self-knowledge, as you so shrewdly suggest. But you've forgotten the relationship of being to becoming, a matter assuredly germane to the topic, and one which many of the great empirical—"

I knew something like this would happen. "Wipe your mouth out!" I yelled. "Wipe it out right now!"

But she was so busy babbling away about useless stuff like the existence of God and the meaning of life that she didn't even hear me. It took an even louder shout to get her to stop describing the neo-Marxist critique of capitalistic ideology—whatever that means—and turn toward me.

"For a minuscule mannequin," she said, "your ratiocination is indeed outstanding." Still jabbering, she reached blindly out toward the shelf in front of her, where I could see there was this little piece of cloth. She grabbed it, stuck it into her mouth, and started wiping. She was still going on about existentialism, except now it seemed to be making less and less sense to her. She looked really confused. After a few more wipes, she stopped babbling.

"Cheryl Zennor," I said in my iciest voice, "you are the world's biggest—"

Her face looked like she'd just been told she had six weeks to live. Oops. I was supposed to be nice, right?

"Uh, person," I continued. "The world's biggest person. Compared to me, I mean. Oh, never mind. Now what?"

"I don't know," she said miserably. "I just don't know. And the worst thing is, I can't tell you how great that feels."

"Hey," I said, "you couldn't have known that the particular drop you happened to drink would have all that crap in it. It wasn't your fault."

"Oh, sure. If it was *you* drinking, you probably would have got a whole set of plans for getting us out of here, complete with maps and blueprints. It's just my miserable luck." Her eyes began to glisten, and she dabbed thoughtlessly at them with the piece of cloth she was holding in her hand.

A piece of white cloth. A round piece of white cloth. A familiar-looking piece of white cloth.

"That thing," I said, my voice squealing in excitement. "That cloth you're holding. What is it?"

"I don't know," she said glumly, looking at it. "Just a piece of cloth, I guess."

"Hold it up so I can see it. Hold it up!"

She did.

It was!

"Aha!" I said joyfully. "I thought so! It's the White Cap! My old buddy the White Cap! And if it works . . . Let's see if it still works. Put it on your head!"

I know, it was a dumb thing to say. After my terrible experiences with that White Cap last winter, I should have known better than to tell her to just put it on like that, without doing some careful thinking about it first. But I was too excited to remember any of that.

"Go ahead, Cheryl," I insisted. "Put it on."

"On my head? Do you really think I should? I mean, look what just happened. I'm afraid of all this stuff. I'm never, ever—"

"Do it, Cheryl, please. For me."

"And besides," she whined, "it has my saliva on it. It would make my hair icky."

She had a point there. Lucky it was her and not me.

"It's our only chance, Cheryl," I urged. "Do it, please. Do it now."

Well, she gave me a really weird look, like I was some kind of evil toad or something. If she'd been feeling like that when she'd read that stupid love poem, I'd be the size of a gnat.

"Okay," she sighed. Then she gingerly spread out the cloth, and sure enough, it was just what I thought—a little white beanie. As she put it on her head, I crossed my fingers and hoped it was the *right* little white beanie.

As soon as the hat hit her head she started to spin. It looked like she was doing some kind of fancy ballet move.

Yesss! It was the right little white beanie, all right. I remembered that happening to me when I put it on. It's a traveling beanie, see. You put it on and tell it where you want to go, and zoom! A sort of cyclone thing picks you up and takes you there.

But as I learned from bitter experience last winter, the hat is just as tricky as all the other Stranger things. And Cheryl must have been thinking about somewhere she wanted to go when she put the hat on, because it sure seemed to be taking her there, without her even saying it out loud. She was twirling around and around, faster and faster. And now her feet were lifting off the ground.

Things were happening way too fast. Stupid hat. Where was she going? Would she know how to get back?

The next thing I knew, this heavy object hurtled into me and knocked me over, right off my feet. The heavy object was Cheryl.

I was looking straight into her eyes. Her eyes were on the same level as my own. Her eyes were the same size as my own. For that matter, so was the rest of her. She was my size, and she was there on the shelf, sprawled right on top of me.

She gave me one horrified look and removed herself from me—as if I was covered with bugs or something.

Well, I would have done exactly the same thing

myself, if my mind hadn't been occupied with something else.

"You wished you were here, right? You put the hat on your head and wished you were here with me on this shelf!"

She mumbled something, but I could hardly hear her. She was still whispering at me, the way she'd been doing for days now.

"What? Speak up, Cheryl."

She suddenly winced and put her hands on her ears. "I'll stop whispering if you stop shouting," she said in a louder voice.

"Okay, okay." I lowered my voice. "But did you? *Did* you ask to come here beside me?"

"I . . . I guess I did," she said, avoiding my gaze. "I mean, I wasn't really thinking. I just had this sort of image pass through my head, you know, of me here with you, and, and . . . and . . ."

"You did! I knew it! And it worked! The hat's here! It's actually here! Yesss!" I pumped my fists up into the air, the way sports fans do when their team scores a point. "I can get out! I can go home! All I have to do is put it on my head and say the word, and I'll be back in my own cozy bed. I love you, you sneaky little devil!"

It wasn't Cheryl I was talking to, of course. It was the hat. I'd snatched the slimy thing off her head, and now I brought it up to my lips and gave it a big kiss, icky saliva and all.

And then I noticed Cheryl glaring at me with daggers in her eyes.

"Yeah," she said bitterly, "go ahead. You'll be home, and I'll be here. On the dumb shelf. The size of a Lego person. With all those poor green children and an angry master on my hands. Thanks a lot."

She was right to be mad. I felt really stupid. "Jeez, Cheryl, I didn't mean I'd actually do it, of course. I wouldn't desert you like that."

"You wouldn't?"

"Of course not. It's just that, well, knowing I *could* do it—that there's a way out—makes me feel better somehow. It means I can think more clearly, maybe even figure out some way to get us out of this mess. You and me, I mean. Us."

I turned to give her a big smile—and really noticed she was there beside me. I actually *saw* her there for the first time.

And realized exactly *why* the hat had brought her here. It was just like before—when she dragged me away from home and into the bottle.

That maddening girl was thinking about being with me all the time. And the Cap, of course, had been its usual tricky self and brought her here my size, just to make sure that the situation would be as embarrassing as it possibly could be.

As I gazed at her, I could feel my face go very red. Almost as red as Cheryl's had turned, and she looked like a beet wearing a red sweater and too much lipstick.

I liked it better when she was big. Too big to seem real, you know.

For what seemed like hours, we stood there beside each other with our eyes on the floor, trying not to look at each other, uncomfortably conscious of how close we were to each other and too petrified to move.

"Anyway," I finally mumbled, as I managed to sort of sidle a step or two away from her, "I bet we can think of some way to use the hat to get us out of here. If we just think about it. The two of us, I mean . . . uh . . . that is . . ."

Jeez. Now my face felt like a bonfire. And Cheryl's looked like a stoplight.

Then, suddenly, she grabbed the hat out of my hand, plopped it on her head, and shouted, "Put me back on the floor the way I was before. Quickly, right now."

Well, I'll give her one thing, she had the right idea. We weren't going to get anything accomplished standing around with our cheeks glowing at each other like two lighthouses, and she was much easier to talk to as a giant than as a girl-sized girl.

But, unfortunately, she didn't take the Stranger magic into account. The hat did just what she said, as usual. It put her back on the floor in her former giant size, and did it so quickly that she stumbled, still twirling, and rolled right into the side of the archway.

And then there was a huge creaking noise, and the shelves started moving, and I had to hold on for dear life to the first thing that I could find, which happened to be one of the stones that used to be the giant Grim. We'd been standing there in front of them as we had our embarrassing conversation. Before I knew it, I'd been flung down right into the middle of those stones. It was like being caught in a rock tumbler.

And then the creaking stopped, and the shelves stopped moving, and so did the stones and me. I raised my head and saw something amazing.

Eleven

Cheryl must have hit some kind of button to a secret panel. The entire wall had swung back. And there was what looked like an even larger room behind it.

It was hard to see in the dim light of Cheryl's candle. But it looked like, well—like a morgue. I was looking out over a room full of coffins.

Except the coffins were made of glass. You could see the bodies inside them.

Hundreds of bodies in glass coffins, laid out in rows. A room crammed full of them.

They were all children. And they all had green skin, as if they'd been preserved in green dye like maraschino cherries.

I stood there in silence for a moment, taking in the gruesome scene. All those kids, dead. Dead and looking as decayed as green mold on old bread. Not even given the dignity of a proper burial. This must be what happened to those kids out in the garden after they all turned green and went invisible to human eyes. Eventually, somehow, it killed them, and then he brought them here.

Well, maybe that was better than being a Stranger. But not much better.

"So many of them," Cheryl said. "So very many." She was on her feet again, holding up the candle and looking into that room with a grim look on her face.

"Let's get a closer look," I said. "Maybe there's something that can help us."

I climbed onto Cheryl's hand, and off we went.

As we walked the rows of dead children, Cheryl's candle lit them one by one, and I caught sight of their faces. They looked as if they were just asleep. So innocent, so calm. So green.

Cheryl stopped in front of one of the coffins. "Look," she said. "Look at that."

As far as I could tell, I was just looking at another dead green kid. Why was this one more horrible than the rest?

"It's Tiffy," Cheryl said. "Tiffany Hammond. My little Tiff, with green skin."

"Who is Tiffany Hammond?"

"She was like a sister to me," said Cheryl. "A baby sister. And look—over here beside her. It's Justin, her brother. He was the next oldest, and an awful tease, but he never really meant any harm." She kept walking down the row of coffins. "And here, beside Justin, is Melody. Next to her is Chiffon, and then Kyle and Brad and Peter.

They're triplets. See, they all look alike—same lumpy loveable Hammond nose. And then Amber, the twins Caitlin and Craig, Wynona, Melanie—and here's Dana, the oldest one. Dana's only a year or two younger than me, I guess, but I always thought of her as just another little sister to clean up after. It's all of them, Johnny—the whole Hammond family. What are *they* doing here?" She looked at me as if she hoped I knew the answer—which I didn't, of course.

"I don't even know who they are," I said.

"I used to live with them," she said. "In the North End, before I came to Riverview. The Hammonds were my foster parents."

Cheryl was an orphan—she told me all about it as she stood there looking down at those kids in the coffins. Her own parents are dead, and she'd been sent to be a foster child at the Hammonds. Funny the things you don't know about people, isn't it? I mean, I went to school with Cheryl every day for months and I never knew any of that.

Anyway, something bad happened at the Hammonds'. Cheryl was kind of vague about it, and I'm not sure exactly what it was—but she was taken away from the kids, and she'd never seen them again. As far as she knew, the Hammond children had all ended up living in foster homes, too.

Except they *weren't* living in foster homes, were they? They'd ended up here in a Stranger morgue, dead, and with green skin.

"If the Hammonds are here," Cheryl said, sort of shivering, "then the rest of them must be humans, too. They must all come from back home."

I nodded, remembering all the kids that had been disappearing back in Winnipeg. If these were the same kids, then that oilhead boss of Cheryl's *had* been stealing them away. It was a sort of industrial-strength version of what the Strangers had done to my sister Andrea last winter. Stealing whole battalions of kids away, and bringing them here, and . . .

And doing something with them. Performing some kind of awful experiment on them? Using their dead green bodies in a weird ritual? Starting a modeling agency for corpses to appear in Jolly Green Giant Cemetery Plot commercials? Exactly what it was I didn't know, and probably really didn't want to find out.

At which point my thoughts were interrupted by a voice. A voice coming from a coffin. A sleepy voice that said, "Keep it down, Cheryl. I can't sleep."

A dead kid in a coffin was talking. I nearly jumped out of my skin.

"She's right, you know," Cheryl whispered calmly. "We should be quieter, Johnny." Then she must have noticed my quaking and quivering, because she stopped smiling down at the child, now to all appearances dead again, and turned to me.

"Hey, what's wrong?" she whispered.

"She . . . I . . . she's dead . . . and . . . and she can still talk."

"Dead? Little Destiny?" Cheryl looked anxiously back into the coffin and then turned back to me again. "Don't be silly, Johnny. She isn't dead."

"What? But . . . but the coffin. The . . ."

"None of them are dead," she said. "Or at least, none of the ones I know. Or at least, they weren't dead just a few hours ago when I saw them at dinnertime. These are the same kids, Johnny—the ones that used to be invisible. See, there's Sabrina over there. You saw her before in the garden."

I looked. Sure enough, it was one of the kids from the garden.

"Today, when I saw little Suze and Ryan and the rest, all of these others must have still been in here, sleeping. A lot of these kids I've never even met—except for the Hammond kids, of course. Whoever would have imagined there were so many?"

As she gazed in awe around that huge room full of coffins, I began to understand it. The kids weren't dead. I'd been right in the first place. He *was* making himself a Stranger army. It wasn't just the kids that had been there since Cheryl came to look after them. It was all these others, too. They must have been changed before she even arrived.

As I was having these thoughts, Cheryl had been walking us up and down the rows of coffins, and I'd been sort of glancing at each of the kids in them as we passed them by. Now one of them caught my eye. In the glimmering light of the candle, one of the coffins seemed to contain, not a kid like all the others, but a dog. It seemed odd. Why would there be a dog in here, mixed in with all these children?

A vicious-looking dog, too. It was lying there with its mouth open, and I could see these sharp, very dangerous-looking teeth inside. I sure wouldn't like to meet that dog when I was alone on a dark night somewhere.

I gave Cheryl a kick in the palm to attract her attention and pointed it out to her. But as we moved in to get a closer look, I could see that my eyes had deceived me. It must have been the strange dim light from that candle, because now I could see it was just a kid like all the rest in there, a gentle-looking little girl with her hair in a ponytail. Not a dog tail. Not a dog at all.

"Did you see that?" I said to Cheryl.

But before she could answer, she was interrupted by another voice out of the darkness.

"I know you," it said. "You there, standing on Cheryl's hand. You're the mean kid from the park. The one who stole my horn."

This voice was coming from a coffin. I peered down into it. And immediately recognized her, green skin and all. It was that little girl whose life I'd saved in the park last winter. The one who'd disappeared in the storm. The one whose house I'd ended up in—313 Oakwood.

That confirmed it for sure. Cheryl's maniac boss *had* been stealing the children who'd disappeared.

This one I wouldn't have minded him keeping. "It was *my* horn," she said in a high-pitched whine, her green lips forming a pout. "I saw it first. It was mine, and you stole it, you big meanie."

"Megan," said Cheryl in a confused way as she looked down into the coffin. "You know Johnny?"

"Sure," she said, propping herself up on her elbow and peering at me through the glass. "He's the big kid who stole my horn. Except . . ." A perplexed look passed over her face as she woke up enough to actually realize what she was seeing. "Except he isn't so big now."

Then she made this huge ugly smile. "You made him small, Cheryl, just like he deserved. That'll show him! Now he can pick on people his own size."

Then a new thought occurred to her. "Can I have him, Cheryl? Please?"

Have me?

"I can feed him, and dress him up in dolly clothes, and do his hair and his makeup, and have tea parties with him, and send him to his room without any supper!"

Well, I've been through some tough times and seen some pretty creepy things, but I promise you I've never heard anything so scary in my whole entire life.

I turned to Cheryl to urge her not to do anything rash. She was already shaking her head.

"Megan, honey," she said, "Johnny's a human being, not something to play with. Now you be a good girl and go back to sleep."

"But I want him! I want him! I want him I want him I want him." She was pounding her little fists on the glass. Then she suddenly stopped and got a mean little smile on her face. "Okay, then, *you'll* be sorry. I'm telling!"

"Telling?" said Cheryl.

"Yes, telling on *you!* You're not supposed to be in here in the Sleeporium, not ever! I know you're not, because *he* told us so. He said that's why I had to be good and not miss you too much when I moved in here. He tells it to all the kids when they move in here. And now you're here, and I'm telling! First thing tomorrow morning when he comes to wake the new kids up and let them out, I'm waking up, too, and I'm telling. So there!"

"But Megan," said Cheryl, an anxious look of panic on her face. "You *can't* tell him, he'll . . . I'll . . ."

"I'm telling, and you can't stop me! Unless . . ." She pointed at me with this evil gleam in her eye. "Unless I can have *him.*"

"No way," I said, and was happy to hear Cheryl saying it at almost the same time.

"Then it's your own fault," Megan said. "I'm telling, and you can't stop me. And now," she added firmly, "I'm going back to sleep the way I'm supposed to, because *I'm* a good girl." Then, with an ugly burst of laughter, she rolled over and pretended to go immediately back to sleep.

Now we were really in a jam. If Megan told the greasehead that Cheryl had been in this locked room of his, who knew what he'd do to her. The best thing she could possibly hope for was waking up one morning with green skin. The other alternatives all seemed to have something to do with not ever waking up at all.

And if he found out I was there . . . Whatever he'd do, I bet it'd make modeling dolly clothes for Megan seem like paradise in comparison.

Twelve

We sat there on the floor in the doorway of that room full of coffins, right under the shelves, for what seemed like hours, going over it all, trying to think of a plan.

The first thing was to get me big again. No matter how we figured it, everything else seemed to depend on that. But there wasn't anything on any of those shelves that would be safe to use to get me back to normal again. It had to be the Pepsi bottle, the one Cheryl found me in. But as Cheryl had said before, there was nowhere safe to say the words and make the person who was inside large again.

"How about this?" I said. "You put me back inside the bottle. Then you pick up the bottle—with me and the house in it, of course—and ask the White Cap to take you back home to Winnipeg. So it takes us both, right? And then once we get there, you find a place big enough for the house and pull out the stopper and I come back to life-size. And then—"

"And then," she said, "there are still the kids to worry about. I'd have to come back here. I guess I could use the hat to do that. But then—"

I nodded. "But then I'd be stuck back home. Because if we were both normal size it probably couldn't carry the two of us."

"Not unless we were, like . . . uh, well . . ." She came to a full stop and blushed again, and a picture of what she must have been thinking popped into my head. Cheryl with the hat on and me holding onto her, clutching her tightly enough so that I wouldn't fall off during the tornado.

No way.

Cheryl clearly agreed. "You could just stay behind there while I came back. I mean, it's really not your problem, is it? You wouldn't even be here if I . . . Well, it's not your problem."

"I'm in this with you now," I said. "The two of us are going to save those kids, and that's that."

"Oh, Johnny," she said, and gave me a big smile—the biggest smile I'd ever seen on her face.

Also the nicest. The way that smile made me feel made me realize once more that the holding tight business was out of the question. The more I liked her, the more scary it was to think about being near her. There had to be another way.

Why did all this Stranger stuff have to be so tricky?

"Let me tell you," I continued, "there's nothing like a bit of Stranger magic to make you homesick for the real world."

"Homesick," she said slowly. Then she leapt to her feet and whooped. "That's it, Johnny! That's it!"

After she'd calmed down a bit, she told me I'd reminded her of something the oilhead had said to her, the very first day she was there.

"If you ever get homesick," he'd said, "just tell me. I'm sure we'll be able to arrange a little vacation back home for you."

When he'd said it she'd just dismissed it from her mind.

"He probably knew I would, because, of course, I had no home to be homesick for."

I looked at her, bewildered. "No home? What do you mean? What about that old couple?"

"My foster parents? How did you know about them? The Cuthberts are nice people, but they really didn't care about me."

"You've got to be kidding," I interrupted. "Didn't care about you? They sure had a funny way of showing it. I mean, after you disappeared they had huge ads with your picture in all the papers, and hanging on every telephone pole and lamppost in Riverview."

It was true. I'd even seen some of those posters way up in Osborne Village.

"And," I continued, "they came to school one day and talked to our class, to find out if anybody knew anything that might help them find you. That's how I know who they are."

"The Cuthberts did all that? For me?" She sat in silence for a long time, looking confused.

"Anyway," she finally continued, "it's not important. What I was thinking was, I could go to him now—the boss, I mean—and I could tell him I'm homesick. And I'd ask for a vacation, like he promised. He'd be surprised, but if we're lucky, he'd let me go. He'd have to, because he promised, right? He'd send me home. But first, well, he'd have to tell me some way to get back, right?"

I nodded.

"So I'd go, and I'd sneak you and your bottle and that little white hat along with me. Then, once I got back to Riverview, I'd find a good spot and take the cork out and let you and the house out, and then *you* could use the hat and *he'd* bring *me* back. And we'd both be back here, life-size. And we could, well, we could think of something then."

"Could you do it?" I asked. "Could you actually go to him like that and pretend to be nice and all, knowing what you know now?"

She thought about it a bit. "I think I could," she finally said.

I sure did hope she was right.

After some fidgeting with the frame of the archway, Cheryl figured out how to get the secret door closed and the shelves back in place. It was a little button that did it. As soon as she touched it, the shelves slid back as smooth as a puck on ice, with none of the things on them even a little bit out of place. You couldn't even tell anyone had been there. Then she cleaned up the cheese sandwiches and put me back in the fanny pack and got the bottle with 313 Oakwood in it, and off we went back to the dorm.

As soon as we got there, Cheryl took out the trusty old shoelace and dropped me back down into the bottle, along with my pink blanket. She wouldn't be able to do it in the morning with all the kids looking. And anyway, I figured I finally deserved a good night's sleep in a real bed—even if it was *that* bed. After she put the bottle underneath her own bed, I put the pink blanket back where I'd gotten it in the first place, and I slept like a log.

The next thing I heard was Cheryl's voice giving me a warning to hold on tight. She was going to pick up the bottle and stuff it under her sweatshirt. She did her best to keep me level. I only fell out of the bed once.

Lucky Cheryl liked to wear those giant economy-size sweatshirts, because that bottle must have made quite a bulge. Of course, to her it wasn't any bigger than a family-size Pepsi bottle, but still—

Before she put the bottle under her shirt, Cheryl told me I had to go downstairs and lock the front door and close all the windows in the house and pull down all the blinds.

Which was crazy. I mean, there were the walls of the house and the walls of the bottle separating us. But you know, being in there was embarrassing anyway. I was glad the blinds were down, and even with my earplugs in I could hear her breath going in and out like a bellows and her heart pounding away like drums.

Then she went to the oilhead and asked for a vacation—right away, before Megan could get to him.

For a brief moment, he said nothing. I listened to Cheryl's heart, my own heart pounding in unison with it.

"A vacation?" he finally said. "You mean you don't like it here?" I could just imagine him gazing into her eyes. What a jerk.

"Oh, no," she said, "I love it here. And, well, if you'd be willing to have me, I'd love to just stay here for as long as you want."

What? What was she thinking of? Had he managed to hypnotize her again?

"That would please me," he said. "But then, why a vacation?"

"Well," Cheryl said, "If I'm never going back there again, there are a few things I want to get. My diary, some pieces of jewelry, things like that."

Good for her. She'd clearly decided he'd never go for that homesick story, and she'd managed to think up all this right there on the spot.

There was another long pause. I crossed my fingers.

"Yes," he finally said. "I can see you must go. Just come with me to my storeroom, and we'll find you something to get you there and back again."

That worried me. Cheryl said he'd never let her into that room before. Was he just faking so he could get her in there and then do some evil magic on her?

But he wasn't faking. "Now, let's see," he said, after we'd been traveling for a bit. "Transportation equipment. Hmmm." I could hear him rummaging around, moving things. He must have been looking through the stuff in the museum.

I had another bad few moments then, hoping it wasn't the White Cap he was looking for. If it was, he wasn't going to find it. It was in Cheryl's fanny pack already. I sure hoped he didn't have X-ray vision.

"Ah!" he finally said. "Clumsy, but they'll do the job. Just put these boots on and tell them where you want to go, and you'll be there. Same when you want to come back."

Boots? There weren't any boots there last night, were there? I couldn't remember any. Because if there had been, we could have done all this without even letting him know. Why hadn't we seen any boots?

Well, the stuff was magic, right? Maybe the boots had some kind of spell of invisibility on them. Maybe those boots were made for walking and they'd walked away and hidden themselves from us. I don't know. I just realized one more time how very tricky all this stuff was and hoped we were doing the right thing.

There were another few bad moments as Cheryl sat down on the floor to put the boots on and lace them up. I had to hold on to one of the bedposts for dear life to stop myself from rolling out of bed and onto the wall, which was now where the floor used to be.

"There's just one thing," I could hear him say as

Cheryl laced. "You may tell no one back in Winnipeg about being here, or about me. No one, you understand? The minute you do, you'll find yourself right back here again. Back here, and in big, big trouble."

"I understand," I could hear Cheryl say as she climbed to her feet again.

"Good, he said. "Then, my dear, off you go. Just say the words there on the card."

"'On asphalt roads or streets of gravel,
Take me home, O boots of travel!'"

It was Cheryl, reciting the poem. Then, after a pause, "To Riverview," she added. "To the park." Good. She remembered what I'd told her about giving specific instructions.

It was just like the hat. It felt like a tornado out there. I held on to the bedpost even tighter. And then the tornado stopped.

As soon as it did, another one began—a gentler one. Cheryl, pulling the bottle out from under her sweatshirt, I guessed.

After *that* tornado stopped, I leapt out of bed, rushed over to the window, and pulled up the blind.

Little hills with trees on them, and lots of paths. A brown river. Houses on the other side.

The Monkey Paths. Churchill Drive Park. It had worked. We were back home again.

Thirteen

Once more Cheryl's giant eye filled the window. This time I didn't even flinch. I just opened the window and stuck my head out.

"You wouldn't believe how stuffy it is in here," I shouted, taking deep breaths. I could see when I looked up that she'd already taken the cork out. "The air is really, really bad."

Cheryl looked very angry. "I do have on underarm deodorant, you know. And the sweatshirt was clean this morning."

Oops. "I didn't mean . . ."

"Anyway, Mr. Sensitive," she said, "it won't be stuffy much longer. Stuffy indeed! I'm going to get you out of there right now."

"No, Cheryl, don't. Wait!" The park was no place to plant a full-size house all of a sudden. People would talk.

But Cheryl was too upset with me to think about that.

"'Make It Grow With Speed!'" she shouted. And it did.

The world turned upside down, and then sideways, and then upside down again. And there I was, holding onto the curtains for dear life as I flew out of the window and then in and then out again, all the while thanking whoever it was that had installed the industrial-strength curtain rods.

I thanked the installer too soon. As the cloth stretched and I came to the end of one of my trips out the window, the screws holding the curtain rods must have finally ripped out of the wall, because now I was flying through the air, with the curtains spread out behind me like Superman's cape. I expected to bang smack into the glass and go painfully flat—but the glass wasn't there anymore.

And then I was wishing that I had Supie's Buns of Steel—because I could see that the ground was fast approaching.

It approached. It approached with a king-size thud.

As I gradually became aware of something other than my throbbing butt, I realized that a giant face was hovering over me and anxiously peering down at me as I moaned in pain.

"Jeez, Cheryl," I shouted up to her. "Now what have you done?"

Suddenly her hands went over her ears. "Ouch," she said. "Not so loud."

Not so loud? She could hear me? From way up there? I reached up in confusion toward the face looming above me—and biffed her in the nose.

Either my fist had expanded, or her face wasn't giant after all—just close. So it had worked—I was back to my normal size again!

And so, I could see from the red mark on Cheryl's nose, was my fist.

"Oops," I said. "Sorry."

I gingerly got up to my feet, groaning. As far as I could tell, nothing was broken. I was okay, except for that enormous pain in the butt.

And I don't mean Cheryl, either. As I stood there feeling sorry for myself, I could see that her eyes were on a level with mine. Below, actually. She was shorter than me now. Her normal size.

The eyes didn't look monstrous now. They just looked, well, sad. Turned down to the ground, like she was afraid to look at me, sadly twisting the White Cap in her hands. Poor kid.

But there was no time to think about it, because I was cold. It was surprisingly cold out for this time of year.

And then it hit me—why I was so cold. I didn't have any clothes on.

Those clothes I'd been wearing had come from the other houses, not this one. Their bottles were still back there. So I guess the clothes stayed back in Stranger country when this bottle came here. Either that or they'd simply ripped to shreds as I grew back to normal size and they didn't. One way or the other, I was completely and entirely naked. No wonder Cheryl was looking down at the ground.

I grabbed the White Cap out of her hand and placed it over my crotch and then thought as fast as I could.

The blanket. My good old pink blanket. It was back there in the house. It was better than nothing.

I edged myself away from Cheryl, walking backwards. Then as soon as I got through the door of the house, I plopped the hat on my head to keep it safe and ran upstairs as fast as I could go, into the bedroom.

There it was, thank God, draped over the bed, and who would have thought I'd be so happy to see that dumb pink thing? I rushed over and grabbed it and immediately rushed back downstairs to Cheryl again, wrapping it around me and blessing every adorable little ruffle as I went.

I'd hardly made it out the door of the house when I heard a voice coming from above.

"That's *my* blanket," it said. "Give it back, you big meanie!"

The voice was coming from the window above the porch—the bedroom I'd just been in. And, I realized with a feeling of deep and dreadful doom, it was an all-too-familiar voice. Please, no, I prayed. Anything but her. I closed my eyes, turned my face upwards, and then, still praying, forced myself to open them.

Another unanswered prayer—I guess I hadn't been going to church enough. It was her, all right. That little girl from the park, her green skin shining brightly in the morning sun. Megan her name was. I couldn't be lucky and get Dracula, maybe, or a herd of man-eating tigers. It had to be Megan.

Cheryl, her hand on her forehead over her eyes to shield them from the sun, was looking up to the window, too. "Megan, honey," she said, "what are *you* doing here?"

It was a good question.

Well, it was her house, and it was her bedroom window she was standing at. And, like she said, it was *her* blanket I was wearing—not that I was going to let her have it back, not until I found myself some decent clothes. I needed it more than she did.

And Megan had been in the house when it got taken away—so it sort of made sense that she'd come back with it when it was returned. As much sense as my clothes staying behind. As much sense as Stranger stuff ever made.

It made sense, but it sure didn't help any.

Because, I immediately realized, we couldn't just leave a little kid like Megan there by herself in the middle of the park. Somebody might come along and something really horrible might happen. I shuddered just thinking about it. No, we had to protect defenseless ordinary people from Megan. We couldn't leave her here.

But we *had* to, didn't we? Because we had to go back to Stranger country and figure out some way to rescue the rest of the kids. And we had ways to get just two people back, not three.

We couldn't leave her.

We had to leave her.

And she wasn't making it any easier for me to think about it by going on and on in that whining voice about how I was a blanket thief and how she was going to tell on me and I'd be sorry, so there.

"Look," Cheryl finally said. "She can't come back, and she can't stay here by herself. We'll have to take her somewhere where there's people to sit her."

Sit on her, more likely.

But it wasn't a bad idea. For a wild moment, I thought about taking the little brat over to my house and getting my mom and dad to watch her. My jeans and things were there, just a few blocks away.

Yeah, I could just imagine my parents' reaction when they noticed that the kid I wanted them to baby-sit happened to be green. It wouldn't take very long for them to turn green, too, just before they screamed and fainted.

Besides, this was Megan I was talking about—and I love my parents.

"What about her skin," I said. "I mean, when people see *that*—"

"Oh, yeah," Cheryl said, her face falling. "Her skin."

So we were standing there thinking about what kind of disease we could invent to account for Megan's skin—not to mention her personality—when the front door of the house burst open. Before I even began to realize what was happening, Megan ran over and grabbed my blanket.

"It's mine!" she bellowed.

I was so surprised I didn't even think to hold on until it was too late. Before I knew it, I was standing there in the altogether again, right in the middle of the park, holding onto the end of the blanket I'd managed to grab at the last minute and pulling for all I was worth. And Megan was holding on to the other end and pulling back for all *she* was worth—which was a surprising amount for such a little kid.

"Now look, you little brat," I was shouting. "Give that back. I need it," and so on. And she was shouting at the same time, "No, it's mine mine mine mine mine." And while the two of us shrieked at each other and played tug-of-war with the blanket, Cheryl grabbed on to it, too, in the middle, and shouted at both of us.

"Oh, Megan, please," Cheryl wailed. "Let Johnny have it, just to borrow, I mean, not forever. And you, Johnny, don't be such a baby. If you let go, we can reason with her. She'll give it back if you explain. Stop, the two of you. JUST STOP IT!"

She'd shouted so loud that we finally both heard her. For a moment we even stopped tugging, although we were still holding onto that blanket for dear life. And I looked at Cheryl, who was staring at me and turning red again. I quickly turned my back to her, and removed one of my hands from the blanket and placed it as strategically as I could over embarrassing places.

It was in that moment that I heard another voice, coming from behind me.

"Well, now," it said, "what have we here?"

I knew that voice, too—knew it even before I turned around. It was Jason Garrett.

As if Megan being there wasn't bad enough, Jase had to show up. Jase Garrett, out for a morning run, wearing jogging shorts and a singlet that showed off all his sweaty big-jock muscles in a way that made *me* look even skinnier.

And nakeder.

For a moment we all just stood there, as Jase gave us the once-over with a typical Jase Garrett smirk on his face.

Then he spoke. "It's an orgy, right? A sunrise orgy in Churchill Drive Park. Jeez, Nesbit, I didn't know you were such a big-time stud."

I was so embarrassed I didn't know what to say. I still just stood there, feeling stupid and skinny, with one hand over my crotch and the other tugging on the end of that blanket for dear life. And Megan, bless her tiny little soul, tugged right back.

"And hey," Jase added, "if it isn't old Lardo, too! Cheryl Zennor. I thought you disappeared or something—and all the time my studly friend Johnny here has you hidden away all for himself."

Cheryl also wasn't saying anything. She looked like a beet wearing blusher.

Megan, of course, wasn't blushing. Or having any speech problems. "Hey, mister," she called out to Jase, as she gave an extra hard tug on her end of my blanket. "This is mine, and *he's* trying to steal it. Make him give it back!"

That was when Jase took a good look at Megan for

the first time and actually noticed her complexion.

He stared at her with his mouth open, so surprised at what he was seeing that he couldn't even think of anything nasty to say about it.

"Jeez," he finally said. "She's green."

"It's nice, isn't it?" said Megan. She held her free arm up in front of her face and admired it. "I look like green Jell-O. That's what *he* said, and I think he's right."

"He?" Jase said.

"Yeah," said Megan. "H—"

"Megan, don't," Cheryl howled. "Don't tell him where—"

But it was too late. "*Him*," Megan continued. "The nice man. He's a magician. He looks after us all, but I'm the one he likes best. And he gives us stuff to make us pretty and green, and we all live in the woods in a—"

Zaboom. All of a sudden, Megan wasn't there anymore. The blanket I had been tugging on was suddenly just lying limp at my feet. Megan had just blinked out of sight. She was gone.

Which was alarming, of course. But don't forget this is Megan we're talking about. I couldn't think of anyone I'd rather have blink out of my life—except for Jase.

Anyway, I've never been one to look a gift horse in the mouth. I quickly wrapped the blanket around me, telling myself that Jase couldn't think of anything to say about those ruffles that would be anywhere near as embarrassing as what he might come up with about what was wrapped up in them.

But the big hulk was so busy staring at where Megan had been standing, he didn't even seem to notice my new bright pink look for informal morning gatherings. "Wha—?" was all he said. Poor Jase. This Stranger stuff was all new to him. He actually expected things to happen in a normal way. He was in a daze so complete it made his usual brainless behavior seem like acts of genius.

Which was a good thing, because it gave me time to try to figure out what was going on.

"What happened?" I asked Cheryl.

"It's *him*," Cheryl said anxiously. "Remember, he said I'd be immediately back there with him if I told anybody about him—back there and in big, big trouble. And Megan went and told. So she must be back there, back there with him and in big . . . Oh, Johnny, we have to do something! He'll . . . Oh, poor Megan! I'm going back!" She looked down at those boots she still had on her feet and shouted, "Take me back, now!"

"No, wait," I cried. She couldn't just rush off like that.

But she wasn't rushing off anywhere at all. She was just standing there, looking really upset and stamping her feet up and down and saying, "Take me back, you stupid boots!"

The boots weren't working.

If the boots didn't work, the magician must be stopping them from working. Megan had suddenly shown up back in Stranger country, outside of her glass coffin where she wasn't supposed to be. He'd quickly notice her house was missing, too. He'd know something was wrong even if Megan didn't tell him all about it—which, knowing Megan, was highly unlikely.

So by now he must know about the house being here in the park, where it didn't belong. He must know about Cheryl stealing it. And he must know about me. I doubted Megan would miss another chance to tell somebody about the heinous blanket thief.

He knew, and for some reason he'd stopped those boots from working. It wasn't just Megan who was in big trouble. It was all of us.

But Cheryl was too busy worrying about Megan to even realize it. "Give me the hat, Johnny," she was pleading. "I have to go and help her."

She was beginning to reach toward my head to grab the White Cap.

Well, there was no way I could let that happen. It was bad enough having Megan back there, let alone Cheryl, too. She was safer here. Even with Jase.

And anyway, why should girls have all the fun?

"Okay, you little devil," I shouted up at the hat before she could touch it. "Take me back to the magician's house! Right now!"

Fourteen

I was back in the same room I'd been in before—the one with all the magic things on the shelves. As I landed just behind the archway, I could see Megan across the room. She was standing there smiling, looking up into the face of a man whose back was turned to me.

"And he *still* wouldn't give me back my blanket," she was saying. "He's a big meanie, and he should be punished."

"Yes," he answered. "He'll be punished, all right. And," he went on in a quieter voice, like he was talking to himself, "so will she, that devious-minded little nursemaid who thought she could fool me—me, of all people. I knew her service here was at an end when she came to ask for a trip home, but I didn't realize how very deep her treachery was. I'd intended just to spell her back and let her stay there, but now? Now she'll suffer."

Spell her back? So those boots hadn't been the magic after all? He'd gotten Cheryl to put on those clodhoppers, and it had all been just a trick? And she'd fallen for it, too, and so had I. We had to be more careful. This guy was trouble for sure.

"But first, my dear," he turned to Megan with a big smile, "we have to deal with *you*, don't we?"

"Yes!" said Megan. "Let's deal with me!" I could see from the look on her face that she thought she was about to get some kind of terrific reward for bravely exposing my villainous crime of first-degree blanket-napping.

I could just imagine what sort of reward she might get.

"No," I shouted. "Don't! Stop!"

Yeah, I know, it was a stupid thing to do—almost as stupid as going there in the first place. I mean, I had no idea about what I might do next, after so bravely announcing my presence. It was like a mouse walking up to a cat, tugging on one of its sharp claws and saying, "Hey there, big buddy. It's snacktime!"

And meanwhile, there was all that magic stuff right there behind me. I could have figured out some way to use it, if I'd just given myself a little time. But I didn't have any time. I knew I had to distract him right away, before he turned that little rat Megan into a real little rat—one with whiskers and claws. Not that it'd be easy to notice the difference.

At the sound of my voice, I could see all the muscles in the man's back suddenly tighten. Then, slowly, he turned. Turned and looked at me.

It was the first time I'd really seen him. He was a guy about the same age as my dad but with all his hair. Dark hair it was, under all that grease, and he had dark eyes, too, and a dark mustache.

And he still looked familiar. I could swear I knew him, had met him somewhere before. Him, or someone like him.

But where? Where had I seen that face? It was there, lurking on the edge of my mind. I almost had it.

As I stared at him trying to figure it out, he stared back, and as he did, his eyes widened—like he'd seen *me* before, too. And was not happy about seeing me again. He frowned and then, all of a sudden, his arm zoomed out toward me.

"Alabanacarandas!" he shouted—or something weird like that.

And suddenly I felt different. Way different.

I am getting warmer, warmer. Cozy. Feels good. I touch my face, feel my fur. Silky. Warm. Good. My paw moves from my furry cheek over to my nose.

From warm to cold. Cold and wet. Good. I sniff the air. The smells are rich, rich. The world is rich.

Now my paw drops to my chest. More fur. Fur all over. Warm. Cozy. I rejoice in how good it is, how right it is. My tail wags. I shake off the blanket that binds me. Freedom!

I drop my paws to the ground, where they belong,

and raise my cold wet nose and sniff again.

Meat. I smell meat. Where is the meat?

"Come, Johnny!" A voice, beckoning. I perk my ears, I listen.

"Come!" the voice calls. It is him, my master. I must go, I must obey. It is good to obey. It is right. It is rich.

I trot toward the voice, tail wagging. The master's hand reaches out and rubs my fur. Good.

"Johnny, my friend," the good voice calls. "Are you hungry?"

Hungry? Yes. Meat. I remember the smell of meat. I want meat. I sniff.

"It's there, Johnny. Right over there."

I turn. An animal. I see an animal. Looks wrong— green, not pink like meat. But smells right, smells like meat. Smells rich, good.

Breakfast. I must chew it up. I must eat.

I turn toward the meat. It smiles at me.

"Nice doggie," the meat says. "I want it! Come here, doggie. Come and play with me right now."

"Go, Johnny," the master's voice says. "Do as she says. Go to her. Eat."

I go to the meal. Blood, blood. My head is full of blood. I snarl, for joy, for anger, for hunger. I leap.

I leap at the throat of the meat.

The next thing I knew for sure, I was lying there on the floor. Me, the one and only original J. N. I was so glad to have my body back that it didn't even bother me that the body still didn't have any clothes on. Or that it had gotten even more bruised and very sore.

There was also the small matter of that awful taste in my mouth. Blood.

Blood. Megan. I looked around the room in a panic. She was there, sitting on the floor beside the magic shelves, and all in one piece. Not even damaged. I was happy about that. Megan was obnoxious, but not obnoxious enough to be put on the menu.

Then what was this taste in my mouth?

I lay there, trying to sort out what had happened, trying not to think about that metallic taste in my mouth.

A dog. All of a sudden, I'd turned into a dog with big sharp teeth. And I had leapt at Megan—leapt at her throat, and . . .

And just as my teeth were about to close, I heard a loud shriek. "Megan! No!" It had been Cheryl.

Cheryl was back? I looked around the room. Yes, there she was behind me, her arm draped over a dog.

Another dog—the dog from the garden.

Of course. Suddenly it all came back to me.

I'd leapt on Megan, and Cheryl shrieked, and then I'd heard snarling, and that other dog streaked across the room like a bolt of lightning and jumped up on me and started nipping. And I snarled and nipped back. I was a dog, and that's what dogs do. We fought like two mad dogs.

I guess that's where the blood in my mouth came from. The other dog did look a little the worse for wear.

Come to think of it, so did I. But not, I realized after a closer inspection, all that much the worse for wear. I had drool all over me, and lots of little scratches, but not a single open wound.

And now I remembered how the fight ended. I had changed back. Stopped being a dog and became a human again—right in the middle of the fighting. Changed back and just kept right on fighting.

Yeah, I was a human being rolling around on the ground with a vicious mad dog. My snarls weren't dog noises anymore, but human swears. And I was trying to bite the dog with teeth that were anything but sharp or dangerous. And meanwhile, the other dog kept right on nipping at me.

What a nasty trick to play on someone—worse than turning you into a dog in the first place.

Anyway, I'd heard more shouting then, just barely penetrating through the anger in my mind. It was Cheryl again. "Stop!" she shouted. "Stop right now, you bad dog! Can't you see it's Johnny?"

And she'd rushed over and grabbed onto the other dog and pulled him off me.

As soon as she called out my name, he'd stopped biting and snarling. And now, I could see, he was just sitting there and letting her pat him as she stared at me. From the anxious look on her face, I guessed she was sort of expecting me to turn right back into a dog again. Behind her I could see that master of hers, also staring at me, at me and her and the dog. The look on his face was evil, joyful.

It was Megan who finally broke the silence.

"So there, you bad meanie," she said to me. "That's what you get for stealing blankets."

"That's what you get indeed," Cheryl's boss said, strolling over toward Megan and patting her head. "And, my fine young friends, it's only the beginning."

I knew that voice. And, I finally realized as I lay there on the floor spitting out fur and looking up at him, I knew that face.

The man I'd known had been old, incredibly old. This man was much younger. He seemed healthy and energetic. His hair was black and thick, not white and sparse. He had hardly any wrinkles. But it was him, all right—the same man.

"Mr. Rhymer," I said, groaning as I pulled myself up into a sitting position.

Mr. Rhymer was a professor at the University of Winnipeg, an expert in folklore. He knew all about the Strangers and their habits. He even had one living in his house in Riverview—this kid named Liam Green, who'd been in my class at school and tried to live like a human, until he disappeared trying to help me last winter.

Last winter, when my sister was stolen and all that other stuff happened, Mr. Rhymer was the one who explained it all to me. The whole thing had happened because of him. The queen of the Strangers had needed to hide him somewhere away from her country. She'd opened the door to our world, the door that had allowed Strangers into our world for all those centuries.

But like I said, Mr. Rhymer had been old then. He'd told me that he was hundreds of years old. And I'd believed it, too. With those wrinkles and all, he didn't look a day under a thousand.

And now? Now he didn't look a day over thirty-five.

"What happened?" I asked. "How come you're not so old anymore?"

"Ah," he said, "but I am. It's just that we all look young forever, here in Stranger country."

We were in Stranger country, like I thought. But I began to develop a little hope. This magician was Mr. Rhymer, and Mr. Rhymer was no Stranger. I knew him, and he knew me. And he was a human being, just like me and Cheryl. And Megan, too, I suppose, if you were willing to stretch your definition a little.

See, Mr. Rhymer had told me about how he'd first gone to Stranger country many years ago, after the queen saw him walking in the woods one day and fell in love with him and stole him away to be with her. So he wasn't actually a Stranger himself.

And hey, he'd been kind to me that time I met him, after I brought Andrea back. Like I said, he explained it all to me, and he even gave me taxi fare to get back home. A whole twenty it was.

So we couldn't be in any danger from him, could we? Now that he could see it was me here, the guy who had saved the day last winter, he'd just let us all go.

But somehow, you know, when I looked into his face, I wasn't so sure about that.

And when I thought about how he'd stood there cool-ly and ordered me to go for Megan's throat, I wasn't sure at all.

"Oh, yes," he said as he looked at me. "I can almost see those questions passing through your mind. You always had too many questions, Mr. John Nesbit."

So he did know who I was.

"That's why I performed that little parlor trick as soon as you made your presence here known. All those questions. You were safer as a dog."

Then his face changed. "Or would have been, if this other stupid creature hadn't interfered." He turned and glared at the dog beside Cheryl.

The dog began to growl at him.

"My goodness," Mr. Rhymer said. "Feeling vicious today, aren't we? Well, we can't have that." And he raised his arm.

Suddenly, the dog broke away from Cheryl, barking in a high-pitched squeal, and leapt on Mr. Rhymer, who was so surprised he simply fell onto the floor, his hands up over his face to protect it. The dog yipped and growled and pawed and bit at Mr. Rhymer's hands, try-ing to get at his face.

And then, slowly, it stopped biting, stopped growling. Now its bark was turning into a kind of whine. It sound-ed almost like a baby crying.

Then, still whining, it—well, it shifted, sort of. It wasn't a dog anymore. It was a kid—a kid about my age, covered in bites and bruises, wearing torn dirty jeans and the remnants of what must once have been a sweatshirt. It was more holes than shirt, though, and through the holes you could see all the kid's ribs sticking out. He was skinny, that kid, unbelievably skinny. Compared to him, even *I* looked like a Mr. Universe finalist. Well, maybe not a finalist.

Anyway, that kid was like a starving kitten that needed to be bulked up—or put out of its misery. And boy, was he ever experiencing misery. He was lying there on the floor beside Mr. Rhymer, his chest heaving, blubbering away to beat the band.

Those high-pitched whines reminded me of something. I knew that kid, too.

It was Liam—Liam Green, the Stranger who'd wandered through the door into our world and ended up living with Mr. Rhymer and pretending to be a human. The guy who'd disappeared the night I went into the sewer outlet.

And now here he was again—and he'd just finished being a dog. It made no sense.

Words were beginning to come between Liam's sobs.

"I—I—I couldn't," he sobbed. "I couldn't make myself bite him, not even after all he's done to me. I never *was* any good at being a Yelper."

Yelpers. I tensed as he said it. Yelpers were those flying dogs who'd tried to attack me and Megan in the park that time last winter. And when I'd gone off to Stranger country, they'd followed my scent and maybe even managed to get Liam. At least I thought they had. But later, one of the Yelpers did something weird—weird for a vicious monster, at least. It wasn't much, just a little thing, but it saved my life. And I'd wondered, could it be him? Could Liam have somehow turned into a Yelper?

"I'm a terrible Yelper," he said between sobs, "just terrible. Jeez, I even rescued Johnny that time, down by the Monkey Paths. That was me, you know," he said, turning toward me. "I bet you didn't even know it was me."

So I'd been right about that.

"I was no good as a human," Liam wailed, "and I'm no good as a Yelper. I'm useless!"

"It's okay," Cheryl said in a gentle voice. "Calm down, now, calm down." She was stroking his hair and talking to him as if he was a three-year-old who'd fallen off his tricycle.

Or a dog she was petting.

It worked, though. Liam gradually calmed down. Soon his sobs were down to no more than ten or twelve a minute.

"So," said Mr. Rhymer. "Another familiar face."

Mr. Rhymer was looking at Liam the way a giant might look at a mosquito that had just landed on his arm.

And Liam was returning the look.

"I wish I *had* bitten you," he said. "You never really liked me. Nobody ever liked me, nobody but . . . but her," he said, looking up at Cheryl, who had her arm around his shoulder. The look he gave her was really intense, and she suddenly moved her arm away.

Liam didn't notice. "Why did you turn me back into

a human being?" he asked, turning to Mr. Rhymer. "Do you hate me that much? Make me a frog, a fly, a chair. Anything but this. I can't stand looking like one and not being able to really *be* one."

Mr. Rhymer gazed at him for a moment, with an amused smile. I thought he was going to tell Liam that he didn't actually look that much like a human—more like a telephone pole with arms.

But he didn't. "Well, now," he finally said. "I'm flattered, of course, but I'm afraid I can't take the blame for it, my hysterical young friend. It wasn't me that made you human. You did it yourself."

"Huh?" Liam looked as confused as I felt.

"It appears that you've broken the spell that made you a Yelper, all by yourself. Apparently it never completely held you, that spell. Your perverse behavior suggests that there was more stupid human caring in you than you imagined all along. And then, finally, your feelings for a fellow being were so strong that you no longer had the nature of a Yelper. You transformed yourself into your true form—the form you have right now. You are a human inside, I'm afraid. Completely human, and doomed to be that and nothing more than that. And so, you have a human body outside."

"I have? I do?" Liam was sitting there with his eyes shining, admiring his skinny arms and feeling his skinny ribs.

"Yes," Mr. Rhymer said. "And you have this meddlesome young lady to thank for it." He gestured toward

Cheryl. "It was your feelings for her that permanently stopped you from acting like a vicious beast—made you human. I don't usually admire that kind of weakness. But on this occasion, since it prevented you from gouging some fairly serious holes in my neck, I'm willing to forego my disdain. I must thank the young lady, too."

He gave Cheryl a little formal bow. "But I assure you, I *don't* intend to return the favor. Your minutes are numbered, all of you."

Then he raised his arms and started to chant.

Fifteen

I had to do something, say something—and fast.

"But Mr. Rhymer," I said. "All you have to do is give the word and we'll go, I promise you."

He lowered his arm, just a little.

"We're not really interested in what you're doing here, are we, Cheryl?" I turned to Cheryl, hoping she'd nod in agreement, as I added, "I wouldn't be here at all except for some dumb magic accident that wasn't even my fault, was it, Cheryl?"

Cheryl wasn't nodding. She was sitting there beside Liam, glaring at me. Also, carefully hidden from Mr. Rhymer's view, she was jabbing her finger upwards into the air.

Well, same to you, baby. What was with her, anyway? I mean, here we were, dealing with a vicious maniac, and she's getting all huffy and making vulgar gestures at me.

But I am a gentleman at all times, of course, and I ignored it. Although, being a gentleman, I did at that moment remember my manners and my modesty and my missing blanket, and I carefully draped my hands over my crotch. "All we really want to do is get back home again," I said. "That's all. Why don't you just let us go? No one will ever know anything about it, I promise."

"There's one very important thing you're not considering," Mr. Rhymer said. He turned and gestured toward the shelves. Suddenly, with a creak, they swung back. And there were all those coffins, glinting in the dark.

The children. All the children he'd stolen, lying there in those coffins and looking like the group photo of the School of the Living Dead Graduation Class.

My heart sank. After all the hard work he'd done gathering them up and bringing them here, there was no way he was going to let them go, just because I came along and asked for them—even if I said pretty please with peanut butter on it.

Well, I didn't know what he intended to do with them, but it wasn't likely to be good for their health. It had already made them look like they'd overdosed on lawn fertilizer. I had to find some way to rescue them. He either had to send us all back home, including all those green kids, or none of us.

He was planning for it to be none of us. There had to be some way of stopping him. But what? Well, there was nothing to do for the moment but stall for time. Besides, my head was filled with questions. I was dying to know.

"Why?" I said. "Why did you take them? What are you doing it for?"

"That, my inquisitive friend, is a long, sad tale of treachery, of the unfathomable depths of evil to which a soul can sink."

Aha, I said to myself, it's an autobiography, is it?

"But," he went on, "I suppose there's no harm in your knowing it. You'll all soon be too dead to let anyone else in on it. And it will be something to keep your mind off the intense pain during the last few moments of your miserable little existences." The smile he made then was especially dazzling. Apparently he liked the idea of having an audience. Either that, or he just liked thinking about inflicting intense pain.

Then he continued. "You remember my darling? The queen? I believe you met her once, John?"

"Yes," I said. I remembered that proud cold lady, all right. She was the one who'd stolen my sister in the first place. It was hard to imagine that tough old babe being anyone's darling.

"The love of my life," he said bitterly, "my long, long life. When I last saw you, you'll recall, I was returning to her, after all those many long years. You can imagine our reunion. It was—ecstasy. Bliss."

But then his face grew hard and angry.

"The bliss lasted two weeks," he said. "Two short weeks. And then, well, she grew tired of me. She'd waited hundreds of years for my return, and all it took for her to tire of me was two weeks. The perfidy of women!"

A Completely Different Place 159

Yeah, sure, blame women, I thought. What a turkey. I glanced back over at Cheryl to see if she shared my feelings. This time, she seemed to be giving *him* the finger. Which he richly deserved.

"And then," he continued, "once more, the Teind fell due."

"The Teind?" I sort of recalled the word, but I couldn't recollect what it was exactly.

"Yes, the Teind. It's the tax the Strangers owe to, well, let's just call it a dark power, a power in comparison to whom the Strangers themselves seem like inconsequential childish tricksters. The Strangers pay the Teind in return for their safety. Oh, that cursed Teind! It was why my darling queen sent me away from her country in the first place. It's paid in the form of a human spirit, you see, and when it fell due all those many centuries ago, the queen was afraid her court would decide to send me. That's when she first opened the door and sent me through."

I nodded, trying not to notice Cheryl's finger, which was jabbing the air again, or the look she was giving me. She must be really pissed off at me.

"I'd not been back two weeks when the queen's advisors reminded her that the Teind would soon be falling due again. And I noticed her—well, eyeing me. I could see she was thinking the unthinkable. Well, she wasn't getting rid of Thomas Rhymer so easily. She was going to pay for even thinking of it."

He smiled again then, and a chill ran up my spine. Mr. Rhymer may have been human once, but being with

Strangers had changed him. He was different now, completely different.

"That's when I started to plan. I made myself this retreat in the middle of the forest, far from the Stranger castle, but easily arrived at by means of magic."

"The well," Cheryl suddenly said.

"Yes, Cheryl, my dear," he said, turning to her—she got that dumb finger down just in time. "The well is actually a conduit that bypasses the temporal structure of reality. Clever, eh? I can be there in the castle with the queen in a flash, and back here in a flash. I created it, and then, slowly, secretly, I used it to bring all of the queen's secret weapons here."

Yes, there were weapons, here, weren't there? All that magic stuff—it was still there on that shelf swung over against the wall of the room. Mr. Rhymer must have stolen it all from the queen. Yeah, come to think of it, that must be why my old buddy the White Cap had been there.

The White Cap. I'd completely forgotten about it. I'd been wearing it when I came back here. Could it still be on my head? Because if it was, all I had to do was think of a place to go, and . . .

To hell with modesty. Slowly, filled with agonizing hope, I took my hand off my crotch and snuck it up to feel my head. It was there!

And then it wasn't there. It slid right out from under my hand as I touched it.

And appeared in Mr. Rhymer's hand, right in front of my eyes. "Like this, for instance," he was saying, waving it in front of me. He'd come over to me as he'd been talking, and just as I realized the hat was there, he'd snatched it off my head.

"Such an inconsequential-looking object, isn't it? I didn't even notice you still had it until you were foolish enough to reach for it. If you hadn't done that, you might have used it at any time."

Then he tossed the hat into the air and shouted some strange words. And the hat turned into a white bird and flew out of the window.

Jeez, did I ever feel stupid. And Cheryl was looking at me and shaking her head as if I was even stupider than I felt. Well, at least she wasn't giving me the finger anymore.

The finger! She hadn't been giving me the finger at all. If I'd been thinking, I'd have realized it wasn't even the right finger for that. No, she'd just been trying to get me to remember the hat up on my head. If I hadn't been so superior to her, if I'd only been smart enough to think about what she'd meant, I could have used the hat and I'd have been far away from here, safe, thinking of a way to rescue everyone else. I might have got help. I might even have got it from the queen herself.

Well, the hat was out now. But the rest of that stuff was there, on the shelves right behind me. And now Mr. Rhymer had decided I was too dense to do anything about it. He'd be less on his guard now. If I carefully worked it all out in advance, and then all of a sudden moved really quickly, before he could stop me . . .

Mr. Rhymer was still talking. "You might as well hear

the rest of it," he was saying. "Especially since you're not going on any sudden little journeys now. That's when I opened the door again."

"The sewer outlet," I asked. "The one in the park, by the pump house?"

"The sewer outlet," Cheryl said thoughtfully. "In the park. In the bank under the pump house. Now I see!"

What was she jabbering about now?

"Yes," Mr. Rhymer continued, "I opened the door, and I went through it and I found what I needed."

"Which was?"

"Children," he said, ever so calmly. "Human children. Oh, I could have tried for some adults, I suppose. But children are more willing to listen. Especially the unhappy ones, you know, the ones whose parents have no time for them, the ones who feel unloved. Isn't that true, my dear?" He turned toward Cheryl.

Cheryl blushed bright red and said nothing.

"As you can imagine," he said, "it wasn't difficult to talk them into coming with me."

"But why? What did you want them for?"

"For Yelpers, of course."

Yelpers. Mr. Rhymer was going to turn all those children into Sky Yelpers, into vicious flying attack dogs.

"It's already beginning to happen. Many of them—those stored in the glass cases over there—have already made the transition from human to Stranger. They are Stranger green, invisible to human eyes already. Their feelings for others grow less and less each passing day. They are heartless beasts now. And some have already begun to dream themselves into Yelpers, just as the spell requires."

That explained the one I'd seen earlier. It had looked like a dog at first, before I looked again and saw a green kid with a ponytail.

So he was right. Those children were unloved and unwanted enough to believe everything he said, to become what he told them to be. It wouldn't take much for him to turn them into his own personal pack of Sky Yelpers, all ready to go around attacking people, treating the human population like an all-you-can-eat buffet.

"Yes," he said triumphantly. "I can see you've figured it out. My very own Yelpers. Soon I'll have a pack large enough to hold the queen and her entire court at bay. Oh, she'll be sorry she ever meddled with Thomas Rhymer!"

This was worse than I even imagined. It seemed as if it was too late for all those green kids in the coffins. And with that deranged look on Mr. Rhymer's face, I had the feeling that it might be too late for the rest of us, too. He wasn't going to be content with just offing the queen. He had gone mad. Nobody was safe. After he finished with the Stranger court, who'd be next? Well, the door was open, wasn't it? The door to our world. To Winnipeg. To Riverview, where my parents and my sister and all my friends were.

There had to be something. Something on those shelves. I peered over toward them, pretending to look at Megan and Cheryl and Liam but actually staring at the stuff behind them.

That sword—the one Cheryl had picked up before, when she turned into some kind of berserk person. Yeah, I could get Mr. Rhymer with that, all right, but not without ending up with a pile of Cheryl and Megan steaks, trimmed and all ready for the barbecue.

There was always that letter with a lake in it. If worse came to worse and I couldn't think of anything else, I could just grab that and open it and drown us all. We'd be dead, of course, but the world would be saved.

Or maybe I could just rush over and drink that cup of knowledge and bore them all to death.

Mr. Rhymer wasn't going to give me a chance to try it. There was a look of cold fury on his face. "So now," he said, "you know why I have to eliminate you. No one must hear of my plan until it's too late. You'll be sorry you ever interfered, John Nesbit. I don't know how you did it, or why, but I do know you'll pay. When I'm through with you, my inquisitive young friend, your memories of your time as a flesh-eating dog will seem like blissful innocence in comparison."

Then he raised his arm yet once more. And this time he didn't hesitate. He began to chant, in a loud deep voice:

> *Powers of evil, be on the alert!*
> *Turn all these meddlers into dirt!*
> *Powers of darkness, be kind, be just!*
> *Turn all these children into—*

Well, there was no time for thinking anymore. Time

to move. I decided to head for Mr. Rhymer. I didn't know exactly what I intended to do, but I figured a good body-check would at least give me more time to think.

As I leapt to my feet, I could see that Cheryl was also on her feet and heading toward the shelves. For a brief instant I wondered what she had up her sleeve—something a little less drastic than that lake, I hoped. Well, there was no time to worry about it. I had to move fast.

I did move fast, and went flying. As I zoomed past her, that little rat Megan stuck out her leg and tripped me, shrieking, "So there! You big meanie!"

It was a well-aimed trip. I went barreling across the floor, totally unable to stop myself.

Instead, I careened into all those bottles with buildings inside, and it was like a well-aimed bowling ball hitting the pins. Down they all went, shattering against each other. And as I lay there in a panic, I slowly started to rise upwards. With the glass broken, the buildings were starting to expand. For some reason, the shattering seemed to have broken the spell that made them small, and all twenty or thirty of them were growing to fill up a space that wasn't going to be able to hold even one of them.

Well, it wasn't a flood, but it would work just as well. Mr. Rhymer's plan would be finished as soon as those buildings grew to full size and crushed him to death.

Him, and the rest of us.

As I rose on my ever-expanding roof mattress of prime residential properties with dramatic growth potential, I could see the scene laid out below me. Liam was still sitting there on the floor, looking up in shock. Megan was also looking up at me with a smile on her face, totally satisfied that I was finally getting what I deserved, and totally unaware of the fact that when those buildings got big enough to squeeze everything else, she was finally going to get what she deserved, too. A pity I wouldn't be around to enjoy it.

Meanwhile, Cheryl was standing by the shelf below me on tiptoes, reaching up for something. And Mr. Rhymer was watching the buildings grow with a look of deep annoyance on his face.

"I knew I shouldn't have brought those ridiculous baubles here," he said. "Never trust another mage's spell. Never."

His arms were still up over his head, and he began chanting something again—another spell, I guessed.

By now, the buildings were big enough so that I was just lying on one of them—lying on scratchy shingles. As my eyes shifted in panic away from the room below and up at the ceiling moving quickly toward me, I could hear his strong cold voice over everything else:

Powers of Stranger lore undaunted,
Come to me and be my slave!
From magic spells unleashed unwanted
I'm much in need of being saved.
May the problem now be fixed!
May now all charms but mine be nixed!

Well, I could go along with that. I mean, giving up

your life to save the world from destruction was nice in theory—but hard to enjoy when you were lying there with a ceiling about to slam into your face. If Mr. Rhymer's chant worked, the spell that was making the buildings grow would stop.

Meanwhile, the ceiling drew near, and he kept on working the spell:

> May the problem now be mended,
> May now all charms but mine be ended!
> End them all at my request!
> Leave mine strong but stop the rest!
> Alabanacaran—

He never got a chance to finish the last word.

Sixteen

Mr. Rhymer stopped in midchant, like a CD player when you push the Pause button. And the buildings stopped growing at the same moment—a good thing for my nose, which was just about to slam into that ceiling and turn into a nose pancake.

It was another voice that had stopped him. It was Cheryl's voice, loud and clear and confident. She must have picked up one of those magical objects, and she must have been trying to use it.

But which one? And what weird thing was going to happen now? I lay there so close to the ceiling that there wasn't even any room for me to roll over, inhaling damp plaster and trying to figure out what she was saying. Something about rubber?

Yeah. *"I'm rubber, you're glue,"* I could hear her say.

Everything you say
Bounces off me
And sticks to you!

Had she taken total leave of her senses? Had all this Stranger stuff finally gotten to her? I mean, we all used to say that stupid rhyme back in grade two, when other people called us names. They'd say, like, "Hey, nerdface," and then you'd come back with "I'm rubber," etc.

Even then, all it did was let them know that what they'd said had really made you mad and encourage them to say even worse things. Why was she saying *that* now?

No time to worry about it. The ceiling had started to move.

No. *I* had started to move. The buildings were going down again. I could feel the roof shingles scratch against my back as they got smaller.

And that wasn't all. As I got enough head space to look down into the room, I could see that all sorts of other stuff was happening, too.

Cheryl was standing there by the shelves, her hand raised in the air, holding something I couldn't quite make out. As I watched, she began to, well, thin out, sort of—like clouds do before they disappear and the sun comes out. She was still there, but I could see right through her.

The same thing with Megan and Liam. They were gradually disappearing, too.

Meanwhile, through Cheryl's thinned-out body, I could see all that stuff on the shelves. It was beginning to move—to dance in the air. For a moment or two, all the things hovered just above the shelves. Then, all together, they started to head across the room. Stones, cups, jewels—they flew together in tidy intricate patterns. As they reached the archway, they banked left and disappeared through it, that vicious sword waving wildly in the rear.

And by the time they'd left, the others were gone, too. Cheryl and Liam and Megan had melted into thin air.

Throughout all of this, Mr. Rhymer was standing, his arms still held high in the air as if they were stuck there. Maybe they were—he seemed to be shaking them, trying to move them. There was a look of intense fury on his face, and he was shouting.

"No!" he shouted. "You meddlesome girl! You can't ruin my spells. I'll end up back at the castle. *She'll* realize what I was up to. You can't do this."

But it seems she could, and she had. Yeah, Cheryl had done some first-class meddling this time. As Mr. Rhymer ranted, his face slowly got old again. Soon his skin was pale and wrinkled, and the arms above his head were thin and shaky, and his loud ranting had turned into a breathless high-pitched wheeze. He was the old Mr. Rhymer I had known before.

Then, still cursing Cheryl with the most horrible swears imaginable, he too rose up in the air, just like all the things on the shelves, with his frail arms still held stiffly above him. As he hovered in the air, his body turned sideways until it was parallel to the floor, and then he too began to move toward the archway. With his arms held out before him like that, he looked like he was swimming. Swimming and swearing. He swam through the arch and was gone.

As for me . . . Well, the buildings beneath me seemed still to be getting smaller, but it may have been because I wasn't so close to them anymore. I'd been blown off them or something. It all happened so fast, it's hard to tell. Anyway, I could see them swirling in circles all around me, like stars floating in a dark sky.

Because it did actually seem to be a dark sky that I was floating in. The room had disappeared, and I was twirling through dark empty space, and the houses were getting smaller and smaller, farther and farther away from me. Soon they disappeared altogether, and there was nothing at all, nothing but blackness and me spinning through it.

Finally, I hit something—or something hit me. Either way, it stopped me from twirling around in space. I lay there in total darkness, plastered against the thing that had hit me. It seemed to be underneath me, or at least I wasn't sliding off it or falling away from it. I lay there panting, staring out into the blackness and wondering where I was.

I moved my hands, feeling the surface I seemed to be lying against. It felt like cloth. It felt like a sheet. I seemed to be lying on some sort of bed.

Not an ogre's tongue. Not a giant frying pan about to flip me into a giant fire. Just a bed.

And, I could feel, not a ruffle nearby.

I became conscious of a hum coming out of the darkness somewhere to my left. A familiar hum. It sounded just like the alarm clock I keep beside my own bed.

My own bed? Could it be, could I actually be lying in my own bed?

It sure felt like my bed—same lumps in the mattress and all.

If it was actually my bed, then the whole horrible business had just been a dream after all. It was like the happy ending to some bad fantasy novel. None of it had really happened at all. I'd just dreamed I'd woken up before, when I thought I was inside that house inside that bottle. I'd imagined the whole thing, and just now, finally, I'd really woken up from the dream. No bottle, no Cheryl, no Mr. Rhymer. I'd been lying there in my own bed dreaming the whole time.

I can't tell you how relieved I felt. Oh, I know, I said before I hate it when that happens—when you think you've woken up but it just turns out to be another dream. And I do hate it. But when the part that turns out to be a dream includes being kept like a bug in a bottle and walking around in your altogether for hours on end and turning into a dog and dealing with an evil professor who wants to take over the world and having to put up with that creepy little Megan . . . Well, I can't tell you how good it felt to know that none of it had ever really happened. I was in my own wonderful, comfortable, quiet bed with actual wonderful sheets to cover me, and I could relax.

A Completely Different Place   173

I wondered what time it was. I reached over to turn my clock around.

My hand hit something before it was even halfway to the clock. Something hard.

"Ouch!" It was a voice from the darkness. "That was my nose! You're not supposed to hit me in the nose, you big meanie. I'm telling."

"Now Megan, honey," another voice crooned. "It wasn't Johnny's fault. It's dark in here and he couldn't see."

"It's really dark," a third voice piped in. "It's scary. Where are we?"

Well, damn. It hadn't been a dream after all. Or if it was, the dumb thing wasn't over yet.

With a sinking feeling I reached out, pushing aside a couple of things. I'd rather not think about what they were, except a chorus of groans immediately followed me touching them, not to mention my ankle being kicked. And I turned on the lamp.

It was my room, all right—my own wonderful cozy room, with all my things just where I'd left them.

And it was my bed.

And Cheryl was in it, lying right beside me. And Liam beside her. And that brat Megan beside him, near the clock. Cheryl and Megan and Liam, the three of them, in my bedroom, with me in my own private bed. And me still wearing nothing but Right Guard.

I had to do something fast. Luckily, now, I finally could. My jeans were right over there, where I'd dropped them the night before.

"Make way!" I said. I vaulted over the three of them, causing more oofs and groans, and jumped out of the bed.

"Ouch!" It was *another* voice. This one was coming from the floor below me.

I looked down. A little kid was there, holding his stomach and groaning. A green kid. I'd stepped right on his green tummy, it seemed.

And he wasn't alone. The entire floor of my bedroom was strewn with kids—there must have been sixty or seventy of them at least, all green. And my room isn't that big. They were packed in there like green sardines, draped across each other and sleeping. It was like a convention in there—a convention of tired Martian sardines.

But not for long. Even as I watched, the green was fading from their skin. Soon they looked normal.

And then, most of them disappeared. Blinked out, and were gone. Soon there were only a few children left—seven or eight or so, lying in a heap behind the open closet door, apparently asleep. Oh, and Cheryl, of course, and Liam Green.

And that brat Megan, who had hopped off the bed and was snooping around, sticking her stupid nose into all my private stuff. If the rest of them were going to blink out like that, why couldn't that little twerp do it, too?

And how was I ever going to explain this to my folks?

"What's happening?" Cheryl said in a bewildered voice. "And where are we?"

A Completely Different Place   175

"These, Cheryl," I said happily, zipping up my fly, "are *my* jeans. My very own jeans. And this is *my* bedroom."

"Your bedroom?" She took a look around. "Gee, Johnny, I'm sorry the Stranger magic made such a mess of it."

"Mess? What are you talking about?" There wasn't any mess—not unless she was crazy enough to think that a few clothes and things piled on the floor where you can easily reach them when you want them is a mess. "Nope," I added, happily looking around at all my very own things, "there's no place like home."

"No place but a pigsty," she said. Then she looked sort of startled, as if she hadn't intended to actually say it out loud.

I changed the subject. "What I'd like to know is how we got here. I know it was you, because I saw you heading for the shelves. But I don't know what you did, exactly."

"It was this," she said, opening her hand and showing me what she had in it. I came over to her and bent down for a closer look. It was a stone.

"You know," she said, "you have beautiful eyes."

"What?" I looked up at her, puzzled. She looked puzzled, too.

"Yes," she said, looking right into my face. "I feel like a total idiot for saying it, but I think your eyes are your best feature. Them, and of course that cute butt of yours. It's almost as cute with those jeans covering it as it was before, all on its own, even if the jeans are pretty filthy and need a good wash. Just like the rest of this disgusting pigsty of a room. But even if you are a bit of a pig, I still think you're really hot, Johnny, and I've always wanted to . . ."

As she kept jabbering on, she was looking more and more upset. Then she suddenly clamped her hand over her mouth and kept it there, looking absolutely mortified.

What was happening? Had she gone completely out of her mind?

Her hand came away from her mouth. I awaited further disasters.

"Of course!" she shouted, looking down at the stone in her hand. "It's this! I should have realized. I am the world's stupidest person. I should be taken out and shot for the crime of first-degree stupidity. Please take it away, before I say something I'll be really sorry about, you gorgeous hunk!"

She thrust her hand out, wildly waving that stone at me.

"What is it?" I said, taking the stone from her and inspecting it. "Why are you acting so weird? I don't get it. But one thing I know for sure, you're not stupid, Cheryl. You saved the day for everybody. And besides, since we're talking about it, I think *you're* kind of hot, too. Nice face, a good body—yeah, a really good body, real sexy. And kind, too, understanding, smart, terrific personality. I used to think you were some weird shy geek, but now, well, I never thought I'd ever say this, because I'm way too young and it scares the hell out of me, but I can just picture you and me—"

Yeesh. I was telling her every single thought that was passing through my head. Every single awful thought.

"Why am I saying all this?" I said. "Because I mean every word of it. It's all true, and that's why I'm dying of embarrassment. Argh, I didn't mean to tell you *that*, either! And why are you so hot-looking when you blush like that? And why am I saying that? Argh! What's happening to me?"

She put her hands over her ears and shrieked. "Put it down! Put that stone down, right now. I can't listen to any more."

The stone. Of course. I dropped it onto the floor as if it were a hot potato.

For a moment we both just stared down at it in horror.

"What *is* it?" I finally asked. "Why did it make me say all that, uh, stuff? Tell all those stupid lies? I mean, you know I really didn't mean it, don't you? Not any more than you meant all that stuff you said."

I can't tell you how much I wanted her to just nod and agree with me.

But she didn't.

"It's the stone of truth," she said truthfully. "You remember? That poem?

> *From lies your mouth be shut!*
> *Just hold me and you'll see:*
> *What you say shall be*
> *The truth—and nothing but.*

While we were holding it, it made us . . . well, it forced us to tell the . . . well, you know."

"Oh," I said. We just stood there with our eyes fixed on the stone, desperately trying not to look at each other.

I was so totally embarrassed that she knew how I felt about her.

And kind of happy to know how she really felt about me.

And wishing I could think of some way to change the subject.

Finally I did. "I still don't get it," I said. "What did you do with it—back there, I mean?"

"Actually," she said, "it was your fault. Remember the first time we were there in the museum looking for something to use? You said you thought there might be something we could do with it. Well, ever since, I've sort of been thinking about it in the back of my mind. And finally it came to me. I figured out that it doesn't just make you say . . . uh, well, what you happen to be thinking. It also makes whatever you say *into* the truth."

"Huh?"

"'What you say *shall* be the truth,' right? So I figured, if I said he—my boss, I mean—if I said he was, say, an incompetent nobody, well, then he'd *be* one. But I didn't have a chance to say he was an incompetent nobody, because he was already in the middle of that spell to stop all the other spells, and I guessed that would include any spell *I* made, too. That's when that stupid rhyme about me being rubber and him being glue came into my head.

So I said it. And it became the truth."

It made sense, sort of. "So then, like, everything he said about *you* became true about *him?*"

She nodded. "Right. I said it, and his own words stuck to himself. And what he was saying was a spell to stop all the other magic. I guess it was those buildings growing that he was worried about. Anyway, his own spell turned on him, and all *his* magic stopped."

I thought about it for a bit. "And all the things that had happened because his magic made them happen just . . . well, just *stopped* happening. All of them went back to the way they were before the spells. Hey, he must have gone right back to the queen in the castle! Poor Mr. Rhymer—not that he doesn't deserve everything he's going to get."

"Yes. And *you* came back, too, back here in your room, where you belong."

"And it seems that everyone else got pulled back here with me—you and Liam and a bunch of the other kids, too. The kids stopped being green. And—I'm guessing about this, but after coming back here, they must have gone back to where they came from. I'll bet they're all back home now. I bet all the other kids in the coffins went back to where they came from, too. But . . . why is Liam still here? And that nosy little brat over there?" I pointed toward Megan, who was happily digging through stuff on the floor—*my* stuff. It made me really mad, and I began to head over to stop her. "And those other kids over there, too," I added.

"Other kids?" Apparently she hadn't noticed them.

"Yeah," I told her. "Over there, behind the closet door."

"Hmm," she said, as she got up off the bed and headed toward the closet to investigate. Meanwhile, I grabbed my Walkman out of Megan's grubby little hands and put it on the dresser. Megan immediately picked it back up again and then ran over to the other side of the bed and waved it in the air, saying, "Nyah nah nah nah nah nah!" I could have strangled her.

"Megan's house is in the wrong place," Cheryl said. "Maybe the magic couldn't figure out where to send her, so it just left her with us."

"Yeah, okay," I said, heading for Megan and the Walkman again. "Lucky us. And the rest? Those other kids? Liam? You?"

"I know about me," a voice said. It was Liam, who was still sitting on the bed. "It's because I don't belong anywhere else," he said mournfully. "I belong with her—with Cheryl. And with you, too, I guess, Nesbit—you're the closest thing I've got to a friend. Some joke, eh?" He looked furious.

By now Cheryl was standing over the pile of kids by the closet. "It's the Hammonds!" she shrieked happily. "Here's my little Tiff, right on top. And here's Justin, Melody, Chiffon, Kyle and Brad and Peter—the triplets—and Amber, the twins Caitlin and Craig, Wynona, Melanie—and that one's Dana. It's the whole Hammond family!"

"Of course," I said, once more grabbing my Walkman—this time I put it in my pocket. The Hammonds were the family she used to live with before she came to Riverview. "*They* wouldn't have anywhere to go back to, either."

"Yes," Cheryl said, looking down at them in a motherly sort of way. "I'm all the family they've got."

"So they're probably here because you're here," I said. "Which brings us to the last question. Why are *you*—?"

I stopped suddenly. But of course—she didn't have anybody, either.

As I could see when I looked at her, she'd already figured that out.

"But hey, Cheryl," I said, as cheerfully as I could. "You did it! We're saved, and *you* did it!"

"*I* wasn't any help," Liam said. "All *I* did was screw up."

"No you didn't," Cheryl said soothingly, walking over toward him. "If it hadn't been for you, I wouldn't have even been there at the end. I'd still be stuck in the park. You should have seen it, Johnny. I mean, there I was, with that big lug dragging me by the wrists—"

Oh, jeez. In my rush to get back to Rhymer, I'd just left her there alone with Jase Garrett. That jerk is always bragging about how he's king stud number one, and . . .

"Did he hurt you?" I said. "Because if he did—"

"That big baby?" She giggled. "No way. He was scared out of his wits, what with you and Megan just popping out of existence like that. He was just trying to drag me away from there."

"It sure *looked* like he was trying to hurt you," Liam said to her. "That's why I did it."

"Did what?" I asked.

"Liam was wonderful, Johnny. He just suddenly whizzed up out of nowhere and jumped on Jase's back and started nipping at him. Isn't that great?"

"Yeah," I said, turning to Liam, "great. How come you were there in the park?"

"I . . ." Liam paused, looking very embarrassed. "I followed her," he finally said in a small voice. "I always follow her," he added fiercely, with a doglike look on his face.

Cheryl gave him a strange look and sidled away from him a bit. It seems that being followed in a dogged manner wasn't all that pleasing to her—not when it was a person doing it and not an actual dog.

"Anyway," she said, "I'm not sure exactly what happened after that, except Jase let go of me and fell over. And I fell over, too, except I landed right on top of the dog. I mean, Liam."

"I tripped you," Liam said, blushing. "I had to—it was the only way."

"Oh," Cheryl said. "I see. Anyway, Johnny, as soon as I landed on him, he started spiraling upwards—flying! I was hanging on for dear life, and he flew me up over the trees and over the bike path by the river, right down to the end of the park. And then—"

"He took you through the sewer outlet!" It was the doorway into Stranger country, the one I went through last winter when I went to rescue Andrea.

Cheryl looked confused. "Yes—but how did *you* know that?"

"It's a long story," I told her. "A whole other story. Ask me and Liam about it some day when you've got a few weeks. What happened then?"

"Well," Cheryl continued, "we flew through the dark for a long time, and I was scared out of my wits, because, of course, I had no idea where we were going. Then we came out into the light again, and the sky was green. And after that it took us only a few minutes to get back to the cottage. Liam flew me right through the front door and into the museum, where you were, trying to chew up Megan. So you see," she said, turning to Liam, "if it hadn't been for you, Megan might be dead."

"I just wanted to save you from that jerk Garrett, because you were so—" His face suddenly changed. "Hey, I wanted to save you! I cared! I'm human, just like you! He said I was, and I am. I care for you!"

Cheryl looked startled again and moved another inch or two away from him.

"Yes," she said. "I guess. Uh, anyway, Johnny, Liam got me back there. And I wouldn't even have been able to grab the stone if you hadn't created that distraction by falling into those bottles. That was real clever of you."

"No it wasn't," Megan piped up from the other side of the room where, I suddenly realized, she was scrabbling through a pile of tapes—*my* tapes—and then throwing them over her shoulder. "That was me! I tripped him. I'm the one who saved the day!"

As I glared at her, trying to control my anger, she glanced back down at the floor, and her eyes widened.

"Hey," she shouted. "Neat!" And she pulled a Raptors sweatshirt out of the pile where I keep it and started to pull it over her head.

My Raptors sweatshirt.

Seventeen

I paid big bucks for that shirt.

"That's mine," I yelled, "and you can't have it. Give it to me right now!" I leapt over five or six piles of clothes and books and grabbed one of the sleeves.

"No!" she wailed, holding on to the other sleeve for dear life. "I found it and it's mine. Finders keepers. Stop that, or I'm telling!"

She made me so mad. "No, *you* stop!" I tugged.

"No, you!" She tugged.

"No, you!" We both tugged.

If Cheryl hadn't interfered and told us we were acting like babies, we'd probably still be tugging on that shirt, and it'd be so stretched we both could wear it at the same time. Which would be a fate worse than death. Instead, Cheryl got her way and the nasty little brat got to wear it all day—*my* shirt, which was so big on her that the bottom dragged on the ground and got all filthy and I had to wash it and the colors faded and it's never been the same since. So much for justice.

After that sordid little episode, it turned out to be a very interesting day. My parents were totally confused when they came down to the kitchen and found me feeding bowls of Cheerios to Cheryl and Liam and the brat in my Raptors shirt and all those endless Hammonds. Mom just looked dazed, and so did Dad. You could tell they didn't even *want* to think about how all those strange kids got there.

Later we found out that all the other kids—the ones who'd been in my room and then disappeared again, and all the others, too—had all suddenly shown up back in their own homes that very morning. Just like we'd thought. And the funny thing was, all their parents reacted the same way my folks did. Nobody even seemed very surprised about it, not even the police or the TV news guys. As I think about it now, I'm guessing that maybe it had something to do with the magic. There had to be something stopping them from asking the obvious questions. It was as if the kids hadn't ever been gone—as if all Rhymer's spells had never happened. Even the kids forgot about where they'd been, about the ointment and the coffins and all.

But even so, it changed their lives. Things are way different now than they were before it all happened, because it seems that the parents began to miss the kids after they were gone and realized how much they loved them. So now the kids get a lot more attention than they did before.

Even Megan's parents were pleased to see her, after we tracked them down at some self-awareness seminar at a resort out in the Whiteshell, and now they're managing to find the occasional fifteen minutes for her, in between their real estate deals. Once they even decided not to let her have something she wanted, and they stuck to it. She's beginning to tell people that her folks are big meanies who really don't love her, and she has a big smile on her face when she says it.

Not all the kids had parents, of course. There was Cheryl. There were the Hammonds. There was Liam.

They all live together now, with the Cuthberts. At first Cheryl was convinced the Cuthberts couldn't possibly want her. That's probably why the magic left her at my place instead of taking her back there. But it turned out they were so glad to see her that Mr. Cuthbert almost had a heart attack.

In fact, they were so glad to see her that they didn't even mind her bringing the whole Hammond crew with her, and Liam, too—who insisted on going where she went. It was supposed to be just until Children's Aid could find them good homes, but it wasn't long before Mr. and Mrs. Cuthbert decided they couldn't let them go. The Cuthberts are planning to adopt them all. Cheryl has a family now. So does Liam. It almost makes him believe he's human. Sometimes he even acts a little human, in a dogged sort of way.

It's a busy place now, the Cuthberts. One or two of the other kids from the coffins are always over there visiting Cheryl. Megan's over there a lot, because her house is only a few blocks away, now that it's been moved back to where it belongs. Moving it back cost her parents a mint, I'm glad to say.

We never did find out where all those other buildings in the bottles came from or went back to. All we know for sure is that they were there because of someone else's magic, not Mr. Rhymer's—which is why he had to say that spell to get them to stop growing. I don't know who or what that someone else is, and I hope I never find out.

I go over to the Cuthberts, too. I go there a lot, because I like to talk to Cheryl. She's a good friend. Well, actually, she's more than a good friend. I'm kind of thinking of maybe asking her out to a movie or something, some day soon. Next week, maybe. Or the week after that.

If Liam gives me a chance, that is. He never leaves the two of us alone. If I do ask Cheryl out and she says yes, we'll probably have to lock him up in a kennel.

But like I think I said, I hate hockey. And the really neat thing about going to the Cuthberts is that Liam still isn't human enough to care about hockey, and Cheryl is way too human to care about it. So now, when hockey season starts and my summertime buddies Mark and Rob and all the rest stop acting like sensible people with working minds and turn into body-checking robots with pucks for brains, I won't have to spend all my time by myself. I can go somewhere where people hardly even know that hockey exists.

Yeah, I have living proof that there actually is life going on outside of hockey. Riverview feels different than it used to—like a completely different place. I like it better this way.

Historical Note

As usual, it seems, the Strangers have been up to their old tricks. Much of what this book reports of recent events in Winnipeg and Stranger country is reminiscent of historical records of Stranger activities in past times.

Indeed, most of the magical objects Mr. Rhymer kept in his museum actually figure in the reports of earlier events found in Thomas Keightly's *Fairy Mythology* (1880). And in her *Encyclopedia of Fairies*, Katharine Briggs tells the story of Cherry, a citizen of the village of Zennor in Cornwall, England, who met a handsome man while out for a walk one day and let him talk her into coming to his house to mind his children. All went well until an encounter with fairy ointment opened Cherry's eyes, and she saw tiny figures dancing under the surface of the water in the well. This Cherry may well have been an ancestor of Johnny's friend Cheryl.

In their tale called "The Glass Coffin," meanwhile, the Brothers Grimm describe a castle miniaturized and kept in a glass bottle, a beautiful count's daughter kept in a glass coffin, and a count's son transformed into a savage animal, all through the wizardry of a Stranger. This wily wizard clearly had a way with glass, so perhaps he was the one whose spells shrunk and bottled all those castles and other buildings that Mr. Rhymer stole from the queen and kept in his museum of the dark arts. And perhaps it was this same wily wizard's spells that Mr. Rhymer imitated when he decided to add 313 Oakwood to the collection. When it comes to Stranger magic, anything is possible.